Below the Darkness

Book Two of the Blood and Hexes Trilogy

by
ALEXANDER FERNANDEZ

Edited by
Trana M. Simmons

Book One: Above the Ashes
Book Two: Below the Darkness
Book Three: Through the Heavens and Earth

Chapter One

Rude Awakening

Something woke Sybil from a deep slumber. Trying to clear the thick fog from her head, she soon recognized Marcelo's cool touch on her shoulder.

"There's someone here," he whispered in the gloom. "Get ready for a brawl."

Not exactly the *Good morning my beautiful witch*, or *Breakfast is ready* Sybil had hoped for. Yet preparing for a brawl had become routine ever since Umaq and Cessani had taken over Machu Picchu in Peru alongside a horde of demons. Over the past week, the renowned tourist site of Inca ruins had been transformed into a menacing citadel of monsters and witches.

Sybil glanced at the clock as she hastily threw on clothes. Just after midnight on this summer night in July, darkness smothered the master bedroom of Marcelo's residence in Avila Beach. Physically and emotionally battered after fighting Umaq in and around Salem, Sybil and Marcelo had taken some time to recover, gather intelligence on their enemy, and plan the next course of action. However, as Sybil's eyes adjusted to the dimness and she stared at Marcelo's tense form near the window, it seemed the mysterious intruder would decide the next move for them.

"The person, or it, has been watching the house for the past twenty minutes," Marcelo whispered. "I've been checking all the windows and haven't spotted anything outside, but I can sense something close. The presence is elusive and thin, like smoke."

Sybil crept near and glanced between the blinds into the large backyard. "We ought to—"

The double doors to the bedroom exploded in a shower of splintered wood. The force knocked Sybil to the ground and slammed Marcelo into the wall. A bone-chilling shriek erupted in the darkness, and a shadowy figure darted into the room.

The dresser cracked, pictures flew from walls, and ornaments on the nightstands crashed as Marcelo intercepted the creature and traded blows in a chaotic whirlwind of fists and feet. Not daring to lash out with a spell for fear of hitting Marcelo, Sybil rolled over the bed and snapped on the light across the room.

A tall, sinewy demon covered in dark gray skin snarled and slashed at Marcelo using long claws. Horns on its knees and elbows acted as spears as the creature attempted to stab and cut the agile vampire. Marcelo countered with thudding blows to its face and body. Reeling backwards, the demon suddenly transformed into gray fog.

The vapor charged at Sybil. She ran toward the incorporeal entity and ignited her body in flame just as the smoke enveloped her. The monster's echoing cry of pain sounded in the room as the mist soared into a vent. She extinguished the fire spell and glanced at Marcelo.

"It could be anywhere," he said. "Be ready!"

A loud scratching raced inside the walls and ceiling. Turning in circles, Sybil tried to follow the sound using her gaze, but the noise increased in volume as the rasping boomed from all around.

A different vent in the ceiling near the master bath crashed open. A long, clawed arm reached down and slashed Sybil across her back. She cried out and fell forward, intense pain searing her skin.

Marcelo sprinted across the carpet and leapt. His arm smashed through the ceiling, and he brought the snarling creature down in a rain of plaster and wood shards. The monster knocked Marcelo away and stood. From the ground, Sybil kicked the back of its knees and the gangly demon toppled over.

Marcelo rushed to lift a nightstand. He smashed the creature's head beneath the bottom corner of the furniture, and its skull crushed inward. One of its legs gave a final twitch in death.

"My heart does not doubt Umaq sent an assassin hither," Sybil said as she peeled off her shredded, bloody shirt. She hissed in discomfort and squeezed her eyes shut. "How did he conceive where we dwell?"

"Grace had mentioned that Cessani has a large network of spies from coast to coast," Marcelo replied as he rummaged through the broken furnishings. "I'm not surprised they found us."

After several moments, he found the herb-laced poultices Sybil had prepared for an occasion such as this. However, she didn't expect to need them so soon.

Taking her by an arm, Marcelo led her to sit on the askew bed and torn mattress as he inspected her back. "Are you all right, love?"

"I believe the medicine shall hurt worse than yonder demon's claws," Sybil answered, trying to jest while her flesh screamed in agony. She winced when Marcelo applied the poultice.

"We can't stay here anymore," he said. "It's time to recruit allies and go after Umaq. He and Cessani are growing too powerful on that mountaintop in Peru. Let's pack and head for one of my friend's houses."

Sybil piled some things into a suitcase. She had realized the urgency of their mission ever since arriving at Marcelo's home in Avila Beach. Yet at the thought of leaving, she couldn't help the sorrow coating her heart. In her daydreams, she and Marcelo remained here to fall deeper in love and share a wonderful life. No monsters threatened the world. No darkness or danger followed their every step. Only the witch and her beloved vampire ruled their perfect environment with laughter, stories, and plenty of *moovys*.

But nothing was perfect, and her daydreams were just that.

Unspeakable evil roamed the planet. Umaq desired to summon greater demons and kill the sun god, Inti. More fighting lay ahead with the world threatened by perpetual darkness; the horrid demon that ripped open Sybil's back represented this harsh reality. Hardship and heartache awaited. But having Marcelo at her side and dear friends like Grace a phone call away, Sybil's confidence and desire for justice soared. She guaranteed Umaq and Cessani's defeat and their horde of demons destroyed or banished from the world.

With clothes and provisions packed, Marcelo paused in the front doorway and glanced back into his home. Sybil read his expression, and feeling the same way, spoke first.

"'Tis no longer safe hither, and I wonder when we shall return," she said softly. "My heart shall miss your warm and beautiful home."

"I'm not going to miss the messes you make," he replied, taking her into his arms.

A dog barked and howled in the distance. Not a demon, but enough of a warning to expedite their escape before more creatures returned.

Marcelo's blue Aston Martin Rapide roared off into the night. Sybil called Grace and apologized for waking her. She updated the older witch on the dire situation and warned Grace to be extra cautious.

Chapter Two

Pins and Needles

Driving north along Hawthorne Boulevard in Salem, Grace spotted an opening by the curb and parked behind a green pickup. She exited the Prius and walked beneath the late afternoon sun toward the corner where Hawthorne met Essex Street.

A discomforting silence smothered the area. Cars crept by at lower speeds as if afraid to draw attention. Pedestrians crossed her path with no words, nods, or even eye contact. The eerie silence and odd behavior not only occurred around Grace, but it seemed that the entire city lay beneath a heavy blanket that dampened spirits and held tongues. People walked with eyes glued to the ground, their steps hastened by unease and a car horn enough to make residents jump.

Kendrick—or Umaq—had unleashed a demon army in Salem and used the creatures to seize the ancient Inca city of Machu Picchu. In one horrifying night, the demons had turned Salem upside down and left devastation, death, and terror in their wake as the monsters flocked to a portal bound for the Inca ruins in Peru. With breaths held and stomachs knotted, the entire world watched, and waited, for the master demon summoner to make his next move.

The old witch, Cessani, had only worsened matters for the citizens of Salem. Her loyalty to Umaq and despicable ways had alarmingly created a cult following of witches in the city and a growing number in Boston…and perhaps beyond. A handful of reporters had been allowed to enter Machu Picchu, and using the media and live video to her advantage, Cessani promised a new era of witch dominance in society. The magically gifted would no longer be viewed as mere hobbyists, frowned upon by the ignorant, or made to waste their talents in private covens. Guided by the Inca moon goddess, Mama Quilla, and the Maiden of the waxing moon, witches' power would rise across the planet and influence civilization in an age of magic.

The Triple Moon Goddess of Maiden, Mother, and Crone had fractured when the Maiden separated from the other two deities. The young moon goddess represented enchantment, commencement, and the promise of new beginnings. Her influence played a critical role while helping Cessani in calls for witches to unite and accept Umaq as an ally in their fight for recognition and respect. The media had regurgitated story after story of Cessani and her coven's ambitions. The constant footage and worldwide exposure had turned the hag into somewhat of a dark heroine for lonely, confused, and frightened witches who had quickly chosen sides over sanity.

At the street corner, Grace waited for the light to change so she could cross Hawthorne and reach the Crow Haven Corner, a witchcraft shop she frequented on a regular basis. She stepped into the store, and a heavy disquiet worse than outside overwhelmed her. The usual loud chatter and friendly atmosphere had vanished.

Instead, customers moved around in silence and inspected merchandise using rigid postures and furtive glances at other patrons.

A ball of frozen anxiety formed in Grace's belly as she realized why. Several witches that claimed devotion to Cessani browsed the aisles alongside other witches that sided with Grace. The telltale sign of dedication by Cessani's followers shone on each of their left shoulders—a silver pin shaped like the Maiden's waxing moon. Tension distorted faces. Body language signaled a ticking bomb might go off any second.

Many people had flocked to Grace's coven after Umaq's demon frenzy had torn Salem and the surrounding area apart. The new members rejected the growing evil while desiring peace and safety. Any other time, Grace would have been overjoyed to have so many individuals in her group. However, the dangerous circumstances rattled her nerves. She had a tremendous responsibility to lead her fledgling coven and provide security. Young, middle-aged, and elderly witches looked up to Grace. Their desperate—and frightened—eyes sought her knowledge, protection, and the confidence that everything would be all right.

But who would provide those things for Grace? Maintaining her poise in front of others while stamping down her own fear and anger exhausted her. Wearing her warrior and mother hen mask, the pressure to succeed and defend her friends had cracked her soul. She slept little over worrying about her coven, and especially for Sybil and Marcelo who had been attacked in their home. How long could she keep this up?

Grace moved further into the store. As she saw the despair vanish from the faces of her coven when they saw her, a burst of courage and compassion surged inside Grace. Their bright eyes and gratified smiles recharged her batteries in an instant. Their love and devotion wrapped her in warmth and provided strength.

She smiled at her friends in return adoration. After giving her companions a firm, confident nod, they returned to their business in the shop. The tension between the rival witches did not dissipate, but for the moment, it seemed her presence had discouraged any potential for conflict.

She approached the Crow Haven Corner's manager, Lily, perched at the front counter. "Hello, Lily. Working an extra shift again?"

"I need to," the woman said in a near whisper. Framed by dark hair that stopped above the shoulders, her green eyes darted between the rival customers browsing the store. "For the last couple weeks, I've been terrified my store will turn into a battleground. Cessani's followers, and your coven, have been cleaning out the merchandise in witch stores all over Salem." She leaned in close, her startled eyes wide. "It's like everyone is preparing for war!"

Grace clucked her tongue and grasped Lily's shaking hand. "With all my heart, I hope this madness will never come to that. Cessani's wicked tongue and influence on television have brainwashed the naïve and fearful witches to her side. I'll try to maintain the peace here in Salem as long as possible. The rest is up to Sybil and Marcelo."

"Any word from them?" Lily asked in a hopeful tone.

Grace didn't dare tell the terrified woman that the couple had been attacked by a demon in their home.

"They are recruiting allies and will march on Machu Picchu soon. We must have confidence in them, Lily. It's the least we can do."

"I will put my trust in them and also try not to be such a nervous wreck in my store," Lily said, casting another furtive glance around. "I think I'm being followed everywhere I go. For the most part, Cessani's supporters leave me alone as long as I keep selling them things. But I don't feel safe at all. And I'm fairly certain you're being tailed as well."

"I know I am," Grace responded. "They don't even try to remain hidden. Stern-faced witches wait for me on corners, at the grocery store, and even in front of my house."

Lily squeezed Grace's hand. "Be careful, my friend. I'd hate to lose my best customer." The woman managed a small smile.

Grace winked in return. "Well, speaking of best customers…" She glanced over a shoulder, then back at Lily before speaking quietly. "Do you have what I ordered?"

The manager reached beneath the counter and placed a cloth-covered box on top. "I was only able to find half the amount. Like I said before, magical items are disappearing as fast as the stock comes in. I must admit business has never been better, but I also don't want the city to go up in flames with neighbors pitted against each other."

"Thank you, Lily. Half is better than nothing." Grace gave the box a small shake and felt the weight of the sand inside. Not just any old grains, but sand from places having a blood-soaked history during terrible wars—the desert along the Iran-Iraq border, and sand from Normandy and Omaha beaches in France.

Grace bid Lily farewell and tried to leave, but some of Cessani's witches blocked the exit. "My shopping experience has been pleasant until now," she told the group. "Please step aside, and you can follow me home all you desire. There is no need for any trouble."

"You are the trouble," a young female Grace recognized said. "Stop opposing Cessani and join her side before it's too late."

Humor filled Grace, and she did her best not to giggle at the teenager, Stephanie. The girl's threat sounded comical and practiced, as if she'd been waiting for hours to say it. Stephanie…the perfect example of a child trying to find her place beneath a dark cloud cast by Cessani and Umaq.

Pity replaced humor as Grace eyed the girl with compassion. Stephanie was confused, lost, and perhaps traumatized by the demon infestation that had shattered Salem's normalcy. Gullible and attracted by Cessani's promise of witch rule, the teenager had found strength and comfort under the Maiden goddess's wing.

"Stephanie McClain, didn't I attend your high school piano recital three months ago?" Grace asked in a kind tone. "Your mother invited me, remember? I loved your performance and told you so afterwards. Your cheeks bloomed red, and a smile as wide as the sky adorned your sweet face."

Silent, the girl's eyes lowered to the floor. Redness flushed her cheeks, just like during the piano recital.

"Careful with your tongue, old witch!" shouted a man Grace also recognized. Rory Martin's upper lip curled in a sneer, his brown eyes sharp and full of hate. "Your vocal spells of manipulation may work on a child, but they won't work on me."

This time Grace laughed. "My vocal spells of manipulation? I'm only speaking the truth, Mr. Martin. There's no magic here. As for you, I clearly remember giving you and your wife a ride to the supermarket last year when your car was in the shop. Are we not friends anymore?"

Grace looked at each person blocking the way, and most of them seemed familiar. With Salem's minimal population—and the witch community far smaller—she knew most witches in the local area after living here for decades, especially those that frequented the same stores she did.

"Anthony," she said to an older man in the back of the group. "Didn't I used to buy you candles for spell crafting when your wallet was tight?" Anthony shifted uncomfortably and said nothing.

"We are finished here," Grace stated, moving toward the group. Some people stepped aside. Others held their ground and bumped shoulders against her as she passed to exit the shop.

Grace's courage and tough demeaner vanished the instant she sat behind the wheel of her car. Having just avoided grave conflict, her shoulders rose and fell in a huge sigh of relief. Trembling, she struggled to fish a handkerchief out of her purse and wipe her face. Panicked butterflies and adrenaline still churned in her belly. She took a moment to focus on breathing and calm her hammering heart.

Eyes closed, she again wondered how long she could keep this up. Her coven, Marcelo, and Sybil were relying on her to hold Salem together. How long before Cessani's followers grew more serious and menacing? Would Grace's coven be able to maintain their own emotions in check and not lash out first?

And where were the other two moon goddesses, the Mother and Crone? Surely the former Triple Moon Goddess deities hadn't withdrawn simply because the Maiden rebelled like a hot-headed teenager. Even if the Maiden returned to her senses and abandoned Cessani's ambitions, the greater threat from Umaq still had to be dealt with. He planned to open a portal in Machu Picchu, summon more demons from the nether, and murder a sun god. Monsters, darkness, and death. Would this insanity ever end?

Grace drove back to her home south of Salem State University. As she pulled into her driveway on Cleveland Road, it seemed the madness was far from over.

In the orange light of the setting sun, three red-robed individuals stood on her lawn. Hoods partially concealed their features. One odd figure stood behind the other two, body twitching in an occasional spasm. Right away, Grace knew the unexpected visit would not be for pleasure. She stepped out of her vehicle and somehow managed to scrape the final bits of courage from her reserves.

"I'm not interested in buying any Tupperware," she said in a strong voice. "You may leave now."

From one of the shadowed hoods, a female spoke in a foreign language. Grace didn't understand a word, but the language seemed familiar, something she had heard on the TV or in a movie. Either way, the threatening tone stood clear.

"Your poor attempt at humor is lost in the fear wafting from your old body," the second person uttered in English, although he spoke in a thick accent.

"You're right, I don't see anything funny about this," Grace responded.

She noticed the pair wearing silver moon pins of the Maiden on their left shoulders. Cessani had more than likely sent this odd crew to intimidate Grace. It worked—she shifted uneasily and realized the third individual behind the man and woman continued to lurch at random. A choke sounded in the person's throat, followed by the unmistakable noise of teeth clicking together in rapid succession.

The hair rose over the back of Grace's neck. Gooseflesh raced across her skin. The single chirp of a police siren caused her to jump. A patrol unit with red and blue lights flashing pulled up to the curb. An officer exited the vehicle and approached the group on the lawn.

"Ma'am, is this your residence?" the policeman asked Grace, both hands gripping his belt. "A neighbor reported these three suspicious individuals standing in the grass while you were away. Is everything all right?"

"This is my home," Grace answered. "I only just arrived and am thankful for my watchful neighbors. But things are not all right, and I would very much like for these three to leave."

Relief flooded through her. She owed a baked apple pie to whoever had called the police. The officer would handle the situation and Cessani's goons would leave.

The foreign female said something to the cop. His eyes glazed over and arms hung limp. Drool slipped from the corner of his mouth.

"Another call?" he asked in a slow, dream-like voice. "Yes…I should go now." He returned to the patrol unit and drove away.

Across the street, an aging veteran named Stanley hurried out the front door of his home and onto the driveway. Astonishment dominated his features. The same emotion shocked Grace after watching the officer leave. Stanley had probably called the police, and both he and Grace couldn't believe what just happened.

The robed man gestured toward Stanley's house as if throwing something. Every window in the home exploded. Grace's poor neighbor fell as glass fragments rained everywhere. In a shout, Stanley climbed to his feet and bolted back inside.

Grace froze in terror as she gazed at the three in red. This was not a confrontation against former old friends and local snotty teenagers. Cessani had sent her best, and strongest. Real danger threatened to consume all of Salem, and more than likely elsewhere. Over the years, Grace had always known Cessani had built relationships with other witches from across the country. But these foreigners proved just how far her network reached. And now, the old hag had another stranglehold in South America alongside Umaq.

The man and woman stepped aside to let the third robed person through. White, skeletal hands rose to peel back the hood. A grotesque, half-rotted face met Grace. Maggots squirmed over pale skin and milky eyes. Beneath a crooked nose, no flesh existed on the lower half of its face. The animated corpse twitched and clicked its teeth in a wide jawbone.

Grace stifled her scream. She stepped back and bumped into the door of her car. The pair of witches laughed.

"My name is Nastasiya," the woman said in an accent. "I am skilled at raising the dead through necromancy. Ironically, my name means 'of the resurrection'. This mindless creature will soon be one of many in Salem, their purpose to control the population of rebels. There's no hope for you and your coven, Grace. Leave town or conform. It's that simple."

The witches in red departed with the mobile corpse following. Approaching sirens wailed in the distance, but the police would be unable to protect Salem. Cessani's powerful and expansive coven had proven that after sending the first officer away using a mere word. The witches' magic overwhelmed Grace, and the dead walked the street.

She moved slowly toward the porch as if a tremendous weight balanced on her shoulders. Hands shook as she unlocked the entrance to her home. Sighing, Grace closed the door behind her as patrol cars swarmed the road out front.

Chapter Three

Demon Moon

Cessani covered her ears as a loud explosion rocked the sky over Machu Picchu. A huge fireball expanded in the night, illuminating the mountainside and Inca ruins below. Another fighter jet had foolishly tried to penetrate Umaq's magical defenses around the citadel and met a fiery death. In the momentary light of the destroyed aircraft, Cessani glimpsed the ancient stone walls and streets of the bastion and realized the word *ruins* didn't really apply anymore.

Even while a battle raged on the mountaintop, enslaved demons worked in a frenzy to stack stone, move earth, transport wood, and pave roads in a massive construction effort to renovate. Not only had the Inca capital transformed to recapture its former magnificence, but Umaq and his demons labored to add a few additional structures and defenses. Outside the impenetrable walls, the coalition of armies had failed to retake the area from Umaq's monsters and Cessani's witches.

Demonic howls, gunfire, explosions, and human screams echoed across the rocky hills surrounding the fortress. Cessani shook her head at the racket. When would the imprudent alliance of countries halt their useless attempt to subdue the greater supernatural forces? Moving down a new flagstone path lined by torches, she headed for the restored Temple of the Three Windows.

The worker demons had transported stone from a fresh quarry and hewn the rock into new walls, flooring, arches, and pillars. The speed at which the temple had been rebuilt impressed Cessani, but the structure lacked the detailed qualities of a patient artist and refined architect. The crude angles, plain fittings, and devoid features went along with Umaq's rushed schedule to complete the shrine. The entirety of Machu Picchu would be restored; however, the Temple of the Three Windows represented the most important project on the mountain.

Cessani moved through the doorway and found Umaq sitting on the stone floor, his back pressed to a pillar. In the light of a battery-operated lamp, his gaunt face appeared exhausted. Beneath black hair, his wrinkled, copper-colored skin resembled tree bark next to all the rock. At her approach, he opened his eyes and revealed sockets filled with yellow, like phlegm—the result of the Peruvian sun god, Inti, blinding him centuries ago. Umaq's sight had been somewhat restored, though the ancient *layqa*, or witch, would never see properly again.

"How can anyone sleep at night with all this noise of battle?" he asked tiredly. "And napping during the day is just as bad while the demons cut and grind stone."

"Why don't you just rest in your chambers?" Cessani asked. "This old dusty temple isn't exactly accommodating."

Umaq climbed to his feet. "There's too much work to do. I'd rather stay close to the task at hand in the temple." He yawned and stretched out his arms. "Anything new to report?"

Cessani sat on a bench. "Despite the clamor, the attacks are actually less frequent. I suppose that's good news as our adversaries are bound to give up soon. They've gained nothing and lost much as Machu Picchu grows stronger before their eyes."

"And not just physically stronger," said Umaq. "I know you feel it, too."

Cessani nodded. Stone walls and fortifications meant nothing compared to the unseen force vibrating throughout the area. She sensed the ancient magics around the citadel growing more powerful every day. The old ley lines sparked to life once again, and the natural energy and spirit of the mountain stirred. Through this mystical power, Umaq would activate a portal to the netherworld in the Temple of the Three Windows and summon even greater demons. Cessani shivered at the unimaginable horrors that would spew forth into this world. However, she tolerated the alliance with him as the havoc-wreaking monsters would clear a path to witch rule for her followers.

Umaq approached one of the three windows in the temple wall, the opening called Uku-Pacha—the underground or inner life. This window would provide the portal to the nether, just as the hole next to it—Kay-Pacha—had transported Cessani and Umaq from Massachusetts to Machu Picchu.

Through Uku-Pacha, a darkened starry sky overlooked rebuilt structures and the dim outlines of demons scurrying about. Umaq waved a hand over the window and the scene blurred, then a light flickered within the stone sill.

Cessani recoiled at a sudden stench wafting from the gap. She covered her nose and stepped back further as a deep growl echoed in the temple. The flashing light stopped and the nighttime scene returned as before.

"The things on the other side of the portal grow impatient, as do I," said Umaq. "Soon, enough energy will accumulate to shatter the barrier between our worlds. More demonic forces will arrive, and Inti will be thrown down for good."

"How do you plan to face him?" Cessani asked. "Witches and demons are formidable allies, but taking down a god is no easy task."

"Not far from here across the Sacred Plaza, I will summon Inti at the old stone monument called Intihuatana," he replied. "It means 'where the sun is tied', and the Incas used to hold ceremonies there honoring the sun god. I will charge the altar with dark energy, and it will hold him like a magnet."

A dangerous look overcame Umaq. He left the window and paced the stone floor in agitation. "As an Inca, I also worshipped Inti hundreds of years ago and only realized pain, ridicule, and suffering for my efforts." He forced a laugh, the bitter mask over his face twisted by hate from a torturous memory. "Intihuatana. What an ironic place to bind the old god and crush him into oblivion."

Cessani couldn't imagine abhorring a deity for centuries, but she respected Umaq's dedication and effort for enacting his ultimate revenge against the god that had broken him. At the same time, the old Inca may have brought this whole affair upon himself, but she didn't accompany him all this way to play judge. As a modern witch, she had her own desires and plans for her coven, all under the watchful eyes of the moon goddesses she worshipped—the Maiden and Mama Quilla.

"I am here to support you, Umaq," she said. "Just let me know what you need."

"I need you to hold up your end of the bargain and fight by my side. That includes cooperation by those I mistrust most, other deities like Mama Quilla. She did nothing as Inti punished me, and the people threw me off the mountain. She is Inti's wife, after all. Do you have assurance she will support my cause and help take down her husband?"

Cessani smirked. "Is there any deity you haven't pissed off over the centuries?"

Umaq waved a dismissive hand. "Only ones that scorn me for trying to help my people, no matter what method I have used. The deities stood by as the Conquistadors invaded our shores, so I defended my homeland by summoning demons. However, the effort backfired. The monsters destroyed Machu Picchu and slaughtered many Incas, but at least I tried." He shrugged. "Old news, old gods, and a former life that doesn't apply anymore."

Cessani laughed. "'At least I tried.' Well, that's one way of putting it. But you're right about the old stuff. Mama Quilla has also moved on and is ready to support you in this modern world. Together with the Maiden, the goddesses will help eliminate Inti."

Umaq shot Cessani a suspicious glare. "Mama Quilla only sides with me for her own personal relevance. She is a long forgotten, little known deity seeking renewal from the pages of a history book. And the Maiden, an arrogant child, only supports me for witches' sake and her own self-importance. The lunar goddesses will benefit when the sun god falls, and the covens who follow them will also take advantage. Those witches' magic will grow, and you, Cessani, will lead them in a new era. I may have been blinded at one point, but I see and listen well enough to realize your own plans. I care little for your ambitions as long as you accept my demonic rule as the true power."

"I've already pledged to the cause and have come this far," Cessani remarked in irritation. "I'm not sure what else you want me to say. When the time comes, I will be there with the lunar deities."

Umaq's scowl remained. He finally offered a curt nod and sat on a stone bench opposite her. Anger melted from his face and revealed the prior exhaustion.

"Any word on Sybil and Marcelo?" he asked, rubbing his eyes and stifling a yawn. "My demon assassin failed, but that's all I know."

"Those two packed up and fled their home, I wouldn't worry too much about them," said Cessani. "Sybil and Marcelo are too busy looking over their shoulders to pose a threat to our operations here. Construction is nearly complete, and your portal will soon open."

"I wouldn't underestimate them," Umaq replied. "That troublesome undead and witch destroyed my original plans back in Salem." The rage returned as he stood in a rush and glared. "Three hundred years ruined in an instant! My vengeance is not only reserved for Inti. With my increasing power, I will eliminate Sybil and Marcelo in the most violent way. Their cries of pain just before death will be a lullaby to me."

He sat back down and fidgeted, his frayed emotions placing Cessani on edge. "What about that other problematic witch from Salem? What's her status?"

"Grace and her little coven are held in check," Cessani explained. "Some of my strongest associates have taken over the city and the surrounding areas. And the walking corpses Nastasiya animated through necromancy make excellent patrol units, from what I've been told. I'm certainly not going to lose sleep over worrying about Salem."

She stood from the bench and gazed at Umaq's once again haggard expression, a blend of lamplight and shadow dancing over his withered features. "You are stressed and overworked, Umaq. Get some rest. You know where to find me."

Flashlight in hand, she left the temple and took the laborious—and dangerous—rocky path up Huayna Picchu, a large peak overlooking Machu Picchu. She may have called Umaq stressed and overworked, but Cessani had also toiled endlessly ever since arriving. Her mind spun in every direction, and physically, she felt spent. Working her way into a cave bored into the side of the mountain, she lit a fire and switched on a few battery-operated lamps, then took a moment to rest on a stone step. Umaq and his demons had free reign down in the city, but up here, Cessani and her witches had dominion over the Temple of the Moon.

Inside the cave, the ancient Incas had carved out six trapezoidal niches, various steps, three doors, and a throne of rock. Near the throne, steps led deeper into the Temple of the Moon until reaching a separate interior cave. Throughout the architecture, the three planes of

Incan religion had been incorporated into the stone: the condor, the puma, and the snake, each representing the heavens, the earth, and the underworld, respectively.

The Inca moon goddess, Mama Quilla, and the Maiden of the waxing moon had made the temple their home. Cessani felt thrilled to share such a sacred and commanding location with the female deities. From the mouth of the cave, she could gaze at the star-filled sky and bask in the moon's glow, or look down at the old ley lines and fountains of spiritual power the Incas had discovered hidden in the mountainside.

"You're tired," a concerned voice suddenly said from behind.

Cessani turned and found Mama Quilla seated on the rock throne. The deity wore her cultural garb crafted from the vicuna, a relative of the llama and valued by the Incas for its extremely fine wool. The richly dyed, combined blouse and skirt draped to her ankles. A glittering gold belt covered in precious stones hugged the outfit to her body. Black hair flowed past her shoulders, and dark eyes like coal stared beneath a large gold headdress shaped like a halfmoon.

Cessani smiled. The fatigue over her body persisted, but her spirits lifted at the sight of the goddess. "There's so much to do, Mama. Things are progressing at an impressive rate now, but working ourselves to the bone makes me wonder if we'll have enough strength left when the time comes to face Inti."

Mama Quilla stood from the throne and strolled to the mouth of the cave. Her traditional clothing transformed into a modern look—Levi blue jeans, Gucci sneakers, Ann Taylor cheetah patterned blouse, and a black baseball cap replaced the gold headdress. Printed on the front of the cap, three different sized wine glasses stood together with a caption written beneath: Group Therapy.

"Even at full strength, you are right to wonder if it will be enough to extinguish his flame," said Quilla. "Facing my old husband will not be easy, but my motivation to do so remains strong. For centuries, even Inti's perpetual light could not break the shadow draped over me. I did not rule at his side, but in the darkness beneath his feet. Like a male lion, he lounged in his own glory and did nothing while I labored to help the Inca civilization. And yet the people worshipped him, the all-powerful sun god, while my strength diminished and my heart weakened. I couldn't even help the Inca when they needed me most. Umaq was at least right about that."

Quilla stared into the sky, her smooth features lost to painful memory in another time and place. It seemed even the deities could hurt inside and feel emotional daggers twisted by loved ones. Her next words, strained and caught in a whisper, seemed to reach the heavens and beyond. "Inti…when all you do is emit light, it's easy to ignore things lost in shadow."

Cessani took one of Quilla's hands and gently kissed the back of it. "I hope my efforts can lift the darkness from you, Mama. I've recruited so many witches in your name, and each person admires and respects you. May the beloved Inca moon goddess shine with her own light, warm and comforting from her heart."

"The shadow left me the moment you invoked my name for the first time," said Quilla, wrapping Cessani in a hug. "You've provided me a renaissance, and each new follower brightens my lunar light. I can never thank you enough."

The goddess planted a kiss on Cessani's cheek, then pulled back with a look of pleasure. "Enough reminiscing of the ancient days. Inti will fade into irrelevance while this Mama is ready for a new world, one with cool clothes and awesome music. And best of all, I have so much to teach the coven. But none of this will happen if we cannot defeat the sun god. If the reckless Maiden holds true to her word and joins the battle, we have a much better chance."

"She can be rather unpredictable," Cessani agreed. "Afterall, Brigid is like a teenager. She'll always do her own thing when it suits her, even rebelling against the Mother and Crone." Cessani gazed up at the moon. "She shattered the entire concept of the Triple Moon Goddess and branched out on her own. However, that fighting spirit is what I adore about her. She attracts so many witches to our cause, and right now, numbers are a good thing."

A bright light bloomed from inside the cave. The brilliance slowly faded and left behind the figure of a girl—the Maiden. Cessani nearly laughed when she observed the young goddess dressed exactly like Mama Quilla, even down to the white Gucci sneakers with strawberries printed on the sides.

"Reckless? Unpredictable?" the Maiden asked. "You both couldn't have described me better."

Spilling out from beneath her hat, white hair dangled to her waist and sparkled as if covered by tiny stars. Curiosity and playfulness shone in teal eyes, two qualities that coincided with Quilla and Cessani's description of the girl.

The Maiden approached and poked Cessani in the belly. "The name Brigid is nice, but call me Persephone. Maybe next week I'll go by Nimue." She shrugged. "History has given me so many cool names, I can't keep up."

"Speaking of not keeping up, where have you been?" Mama Quilla chided. "Umaq nearly collapsed from the strain of rebuilding this place and fighting off mortals. Cessani is struggling to tap magic from the ley lines and spiritual fountains around the mountain. And I've been traveling the world, appearing before witches and preparing them for what's to come." She glared at Persephone's outfit. "Besides finding time to mock me, what have you done to prepare for Inti?"

"Oh, just some CrossFit and Pilates to build my strength." The young goddess flexed a bicep, a fist near her ear. "Bring it on!"

Quilla uttered an exasperated sigh. "I swear I will throttle you, child. If you're not going to take this seriously, then don't come here anymore."

"Well, that was harsh," Persephone replied. "If I leave, then you won't be able to use these."

She reached in a pocket and threw some clear, jagged stones into the air. The glittering objects floated in a slow circle between the women.

"Crystalized moon dust," Cessani observed in astonishment. "These will be like bullets against the sun god."

"Just like Mama, I've also been traveling," said Persephone. "Only to much farther and lonelier places." She glanced up at the moon. "And too damn cold!"

Quilla yanked the bill of the Maiden's hat down over the girl's face. "Not bad for an immature brat. You are still reckless, but I give you points for this."

Persephone fixed her hat, then lifted her chin and sniffed once holding a mock look of arrogance. "When I reach one hundred points, you owe me a Snickers." After a moment, the haughty mask vanished and she appeared serious. "I've already broken the Triple Goddess archetype. What happens to the world's natural mystical order when the sun god falls? Will the unbalanced energy be too much? Are we making a mistake siding with Umaq?"

"Very good questions, ones Cessani and I have discussed at length," Quilla responded. "If you were around more, you'd have learned a thing or two." Persephone smirked. Quilla shook her head in irritation, then gestured to Cessani. "Care to explain to the child?"

Cessani suppressed a smile at the two bickering deities. "There have been many sun gods throughout history," she began. "Tawa, Ah Kin, Ra, Guaraci, and Nanahuatzin just to name a few. Extinguishing the light of one deity will indeed have an effect on the world's natural balance, but not enough to cause peril as long as the other sun gods exist. Once Inti is gone, the lunar energy will grow more potent. For the most part, only supernatural beings will sense the real change and be affected by it. Witches, for example, will experience a boost in their abilities as long as they call upon the Maiden and Mama Quilla."

Persephone gave a thumbs up. "Then I'm in!" She stretched out an arm, and the swirling crystals returned to her hand. She slipped them into a pocket, then turned and walked back into the cave. "Call me when the first punch is thrown."

Quilla lifted a hand in protest as the young goddess moved further inside. About to speak to Persephone's back, she dropped her arm and sighed.

"If that was a promise of commitment by the Maiden, then I'll take it," she said wearily.

"Reckless and unpredictable," said Cessani. "But I trust her on this one." She nodded to Quilla. "A god will fall and witches will rise, Mama. Normal humans will submit to us and bestow the respect witches deserve. Our magic is not a living room hobby meant for entertaining curious people, or for petty fortunetelling and trinkets. Our status has fallen over the centuries, and I'm here to rekindle the spirits of old and restore the ancient ways. Umaq can have his demons and call it rule, but the moon goddesses and witches will have their own power and prestige."

Energetic clapping sounded from within the cave. Apparently, the Maiden had remained close enough to eavesdrop.

Chapter Four

Wannabe and Wolf

Cruising about an hour northeast of Sacramento, Marcelo pulled off the highway and into Nevada City, a historical location with a population around three thousand. At five o'clock in the morning, Sybil should have been dead asleep in the passenger seat, but the significance of this journey kept her eyes open. The battle against Umaq and Cessani required allies, and hopefully Marcelo would be able to persuade one of his acquaintances to join. The Aston Martin turned right onto Boulder Road, and Sybil listened in interest after asking Marcelo to explain more about her surroundings.

First settled in 1849 during the California Gold Rush, Nevada City became one of the most important mining towns in the state. The name Nevada means "snow-covered" and referred to the snow-capped mountains in the region. Several years after the first settlements grew, the word "City" was added to the name to eliminate confusion with the neighboring state of Nevada. Now a thriving tourist spot, the city contained several municipal buildings, which remain part of the National Register of Historic Places. The town also housed many popular antique dealers, fine restaurants, and quaint bed and breakfasts, one of which happened to be their destination.

Sybil would have loved to see the city during daylight and play tourist, but reality returned once Marcelo parked in front of the Fang and Howl Bed & Breakfast. She stepped out of the car and zipped up her coat against the early morning chill. Walking down a flagstone path toward the entrance, she observed the sign and looked forward to meeting her first werewolf.

"Ok," Marcelo whispered once they ascended a few steps to the wooden porch. "As owner of this place, Johann is sort of a neat freak, so make sure there's no mud on your sh—"

"Let's just go with 'freak'," a voice said from a darkened corner.

Sybil's heart jumped, and Marcelo appeared startled. A chain rattled, wood creaked, and a middle-aged man stepped out of the shadows. His blond hair hung in a ponytail, long bangs hanging on each side of his face. Dark eyes, nearly black in the low light, glittered above a smile. Behind him, Sybil caught the outline of a porch swing as it rocked lazily. The man had probably been watching them ever since the car pulled up.

"Johann, you're awake," Marcelo said, returning the smile. The two friends embraced and exchanged claps on the back.

"Of course I'm up," Johann replied. "As a werewolf, I have a sensitive canine nose, remember? The closer you got, the stronger your rotten, undead stench became. Who could sleep through that?" He glanced past Marcelo's shoulder. "Certainly not that slender beauty behind you."

"You speak true, I warrant," Sybil agreed. "Marcelo's showers are never enough."

Johann laughed, and Marcelo shook his head. "Johann, meet my beloved and the most powerful witch on the planet."

Sybil grinned and extended her hand. "Sybil Radella Cotterill."

Johann frowned at her outstretched arm. "When it's the end of the world according to the news, only hugs are given here." He then winked and embraced Sybil. "Johann Fischer. Welcome to my bed and breakfast, most powerful witch on the planet."

He turned to Marcelo. "Your frantic text had me awake all night, so I only have a partial story since you refused to call. Let's go inside and talk before the sun comes up and turns you to ash on my porch. Then I'd have to clean. I am a neat freak, after all."

They moved inside, and Johann quietly closed the door. "Three of the five rooms are occupied by guests," he whispered. "Let's head over to the master bedroom."

A bright light in the adjoining kitchen partially illuminated the entry and living room. Impressed by the décor, Sybil loved the wood flooring with flower-pattered rugs and large brick fireplace. Tufted, rose-colored sofas and love seats surrounded a wide oak table, gilded candlesticks on top. Paintings of nature scenes lined the walls, and a huge iron chandelier hung beneath exposed rafters in the high ceiling.

Crossing the living room, Sybil peered into a dim dining area next to the kitchen, where several tables and chairs sat. She imagined the seats filled with travelers from all around, smiling and talking over hot breakfast and steaming cocoa or coffee. How she would love to travel like them and visit new places. She pictured snuggling against Marcelo on the plush sofa, the fireplace blazing and warm on her skin. Wine glasses in hand, they exchanged stories and sightseeing tips with other explorers.

After walking down a long hallway lined by electric lights shaped like torches, Johann opened a set of double doors and stepped into an enormous master bedroom. He snapped on the light, and Sybil shrieked in surprise at a man in undergarments sprawled on the bed.

Johann scowled and slapped the man on his rear, then nudged the mattress several times using a bare foot. "Dom, I told you to be awake and ready for our visitors. Get up. Your punishment is to go and make coffee."

Dom moaned into a pillow, then slowly crawled off the bed, his brown hair mussed. Eyes squinted against the light, he struggled into a pair of sweats and threw on a robe.

"Hi, Marcelo," he said through a yawn. He offered Sybil a lazy wave. "Young lady, I'll greet you properly after three cups of coffee." Heading for the door, Dom returned a hard swat to Johann's rear in an act of revenge.

"Pathetic," Johann mumbled after Dom left. He motioned to a couch. "Let the chat begin."

Cheeks still flushed from watching the intimate exchange, Sybil finally had a moment to admire the spacious bedroom as she went to sit. Similar to the living room, a wide brick fireplace dominated one side of the area. Colorful red, white, and yellow thorned roses decorated a lively rug. Paintings of angelic figures and gothic castles hung on the wood-paneled walls. Two tall wardrobes and a matching vanity sat opposite the fireplace. The room smelled wonderful, and Sybil didn't see a speck of dust or discarded article of clothing anywhere.

The three spoke at length until Johann seemed satisfied, his questions answered. "Well, I'm very impressed by what you two have been through." He leaned back in a plush chair. "I've kept up with the news, and I suppose those demons and witches are somewhat of an annoyance." He chuckled and shook his head. "And to think my old vampire friend is caught right in the middle. Now you wish to drag me into the mess?" He studied a beautiful grandfather clock near the vanity. "I'll have to think about it."

The doors suddenly opened. "Coward," Dom said as he entered using long strides. His robe swirled, and intense green eyes fixed on Johann. Beneath disheveled hair, Dom's smooth face seemed much more alert than before. "I enjoyed my three cups of coffee while listening at the door. There's nothing to think about, and you know it. Go and help your friends. I am perfectly capable of running the bed and breakfast alone."

Dom turned to Sybil and bowed. "My apologies. My name is Dominic Rossi, a perfectly normal human shacked up with a silly pet werewolf."

Sybil stood from the sofa and introduced herself, then hugged Dominic. "With the end of the world, only hugs shall be given here. Thereof some wonderful advice from yonder silly pet werewolf." She smiled at Johann.

Johann stood up and crossed his arms. "I'm surrounded by comedians. And I'm definitely no coward," he spat at Dom. "Merely cautious." He faced

Marcelo and nodded. "I will help, of course. You wanted some extra muscle? Then I'm your dog. As for the bed and breakfast, Dom is nowhere near the cook I am, but…" He gazed at Dom in adoration. "He's a real ace at running this joint, and there's no one else on earth I trust more."

A returned love shone in Dom's gaze. "If you'll excuse me, I must get dressed and start breakfast for our house guests," he said to the group. "Sybil, you are more than welcome to partake." He turned and headed for the washroom.

"Sybil might enjoy eggs and pancakes, but Marcelo, you need something else," Johann remarked. "You need to drink. I can smell it in your complexion." He stepped forward and patted his wrist. "This wouldn't be the first time I've offered my extra spicy werewolf blood. And I know you—don't be bashful or polite. Just take it before I punch you."

Sybil laughed. "Of a truth, you conceive him very well indeed, Johann. Hitherto, Marcelo still hesitates when I offer my blood at home. He hath behaved like a shy teenager with his first kiss. I have not had to punch him yet, I warrant."

Marcelo closed his eyes and sighed. "I dislike you both." He then glanced at Johann and took hold of the outstretched arm. "Your supernatural blood does have a nice kick, I'll admit."

Marcelo bit into Johann's flesh and drank. Afterwards, he sat back on the sofa and appeared very satisfied, similar to how Sybil felt when polishing off a bacon cheeseburger and fries.

Johann licked the bite area on his wrist, and the puncture wounds sealed. "A vampire who is not a vampire. Having a soul—demon or otherwise—makes you different than traditional blood drinkers. I've always wondered, Marcelo, does that ever make you feel…I don't know. Out of place?"

Marcelo's cool hand grasped Sybil's, and she scooted closer to him. "The demon spirit Umaq placed inside my dead body requires blood," he began. "If I don't drink, I die. But that's the only thing I share with *real* vampires. Those beings don't have a soul at all. I also wasn't bitten, turned, sired, or whatever you call the process of becoming an undead. So am I classified as a vampire? I have similar characteristics, and Umaq nearly forced me to turn Sybil into one after bewitching me. But at the same time, I am different." He shrugged. "To answer your question, my shaggy friend, I do feel out of place. But that's just the way my life is. No big deal."

Grief touched Sybil as she studied the side of Marcelo's face. *No big deal*. That's what he said, but the distant look in his gaze, his tone, and the silence of his unbeating heart told a different story. Johann's question bothered him. While explaining, it seemed Marcelo struggled to say so much more, to justify his existence. However, no words sounded genuine as he provided a hollow answer. She squeezed his hand that had started to warm in her grip. A simple gesture, but one filled by her love and support.

"You're a castoff, a wannabe vampire," Johann said wearing a smirk. "But we love you just the same."

"I appreciate your mush," Marcelo replied. "Since we're being so sweet to each other, Sybil wanted to ask you some questions about the werewolf life. She'd love to know more about you."

Johann smiled with delight in his dark eyes. "Really? Well, Sybil, you're in luck because I do enjoy bragging. Please, ask away."

Excited to finally learn more about him, Sybil leaned forward on the sofa. "You are the first werewolf I have actually met, I warrant. In my time agone during the seventeenth century, the werewolves—"

"Whoa, wait a sec!" Johann exclaimed. "The seventeenth century? Girl, you're going to have to share your story with me later." He glanced at Marcelo. "She's gorgeous and apparently has an extremely interesting history. Don't let this one go."

"I don't plan to," Marcelo said, draping an arm around her.

Johann made himself more comfortable on the chair. "Sorry, Sybil. Please continue."

"Hitherto, I had conceived that werewolves were wild and ferocious creatures," she began. "While transformed, they may kill in uncontrolled rages, though only during a full moon. Strive as they might, those individuals could not resist the alteration and had no memory of what horror they might have done." She looked at the floor, ashamed. "I beg your pardon if what I conceived is hearsay, as I have not had a fair sight of werewolves."

"Nothing to worry about," Johann responded. "As for the seventeenth century, your information is accurate. Werewolf transformations were indeed savage and irrepressible. Men and women would wake up in strange places with blood staining their hands and mouths, not having any idea where they'd been or what had happened."

He gestured toward Marcelo. "But like the vampires, werewolves had to adapt over the centuries to modernization and improvements in society. My kind didn't adapt because we enjoyed sipping tea and nibbling crumpets with normal people. It became a matter of survival, you see. The violent, unchecked beasts were hunted. Those that discovered how to control transformations, be conscious of their actions, and master the sway of the moon…lived."

"Truly, how was the control accomplished?" Sybil asked, intrigued. "I imagine a sundry of strong magics were involved."

"Some people were able to find the answer with shamans, witches, or using voodoo," Johann answered. "Others studied and practiced on their own using books of the occult. Lastly, some learned through guided meditation. None of those methods are quick and easy, however. My family in Germany practiced the latter and passed their knowledge onward through the generations."

"You are truly remarkable, Johann," Sybil commented. "It pleases me to learn such an astonishing history. Thus, you can change at will and on any night of the month?"

Johann nodded. "And here's the bonus—I can also convert during the day. But our connection to the moon is forever present, which means my werewolf form is weaker in daylight and I cannot hold it for long."

"Don't let him fool you, Sybil," Marcelo cut in. "Johann is weak no matter what. All that bark and no bite. He's just a trained puppy."

"I'm not as weak as your insult, fang boy," Johann countered. "But in a way, I suppose we did train ourselves. However, there are still feral werewolves roaming about. They haven't been able to adapt or choose not to. Those stories about people chaining themselves in cages during the full moon are true. And others don't care to restrain themselves at all or worry about what happens during their blind transformation."

Johann checked the grandfather clock. "I'm going to help Dom with breakfast before the early bird guests wake. Shouldn't take much longer." He closed the thick velvet window curtains, then clapped Marcelo on the shoulder. "Sun will be up soon. You two relax in here for a bit. I'll bring your breakfast, Sybil."

She thanked Johann as he left, then studied Marcelo's somber face. "I conceive there is more you desired to say about being out of place, my dear." She cupped his smooth cheek and caressed his bottom lip with a thumb. "Tell me how you truly feel, Marcelo. There is trouble inside that ails you, and I wish to remedy it."

He gently took her hand and kissed the palm. Holding her hand between his, he stared across the room, his expression in a faraway place. "I have been lost for centuries, Sybil. I traveled the world searching for someone else like me, or for someone who could explain where I belonged in the supernatural order. But back in Salem, when I saw Umaq again after five hundred years, I realized the explanation for my existence is actually quite simple."

He forced a small laugh. "Umaq is a master demon summoner, and I'm nothing more than a failed experiment. I'll never forget the circumstances of my death. I told you my story, how Umaq called forth a demon through a portal of fire and commanded it to slay me. The monster and I died, then Umaq bound the demon's spirit inside my body. He tried to control me like the demon but couldn't, so I fled. And that is my existence—an unfinished, exploratory, and nameless creature with no purpose except to feed on innocent blood."

"The demon feeds, Marcelo, not you," Sybil said quietly. "Your memories, emotions, and human conscience remaineth. Hitherto, that makes you human, the young man from Spain I am very grateful to have met. Thereof you are no experiment, but the person I fell in love with. It matters not what actions you perform out of necessity and survival. It does not mean yonder demon hath taken control of you."

Marcelo leaned in and placed a tender kiss on her forehead. "That may be, my love, but it's just so hard sometimes. My body is a constant battlefield, torn between a human consciousness and a malevolent demon spirit that only desires rampant slaughter. I hear it sometimes, Sybil. The demon *hates* me. It's first words were, 'Your flesh and bone are mine, mortal'. The monster seemed content with possession, but now it sees me as weak and useless while I manage the feedings."

Marcelo placed a hand over his chest. "I can feel the demonic essence either trying to burst out and escape or stay inside and manipulate me. I suppose Umaq not only destroyed my existence, but the demon's as well. No wonder the spirit is angry."

"Do not feel as if you must strive against the demon alone, Marcelo. We shall do it together. I am always here for you and shall do whatever it takes to keep the beast subdued." Sybil smiled. "Do not forget what you said on yonder porch. I am the most powerful witch on the planet, remember?"

Marcelo returned the smile, and joy filled her when the desolation from before vanished from his face. "I'm also the luckiest man on the planet to have found you."

His arms slipped around her, and she melted into the embrace. Passion fueled their fiery kiss as her heart thundered. In the heat of the moment, Sybil imagined borrowing Johann's bed. But just then, the blond man entered and interrupted the pair with unfortunate timing.

"I knew you two kids couldn't be left alone," Johann observed. "I apologize for the intrusion, but I guess you're returning the favor after seeing Dom half-naked on the bed." He placed a tray of scrambled eggs, sausage, toast, and pancakes on a small table.

"That food is a fair sight, I warrant," said Sybil. "It smells wonderful."

"There's plenty more if you finish this," Johann offered. "Marcelo, I don't believe I'm the only fool you called upon to join this Umaq-hunting quest. So, who else have you suckered?"

"You're the first sucker," Marcelo answered. "The next will hopefully be Salix."

Johann's eyebrows rose. "Our little plant face? You're really building a team of varied talents, I see. She can certainly hold her own. When are we leaving?"

"We'll leave at sundown," Marcelo replied. "Should provide enough time to prepare, rest, and say proper farewells."

Johann opened a drawer in the vanity and threw Marcelo a key. "Room four is all yours until we leave." He studied them, a knowing grin on his face. "After seeing what I walked in on, I'm sure you two have some unfinished business to take care of before hitting the road again."

Sybil devoured the delicious breakfast and enjoyed a cup of hot coffee. Afterwards, she took the key from Marcelo and led him to the door of room four.

"Unfinished business," she whispered in his ear before pulling him inside.

Chapter Five

Uprooted Silence

Heading north on the I-5 freeway, Marcelo drove past the California border and into southern Oregon. He glanced at the passenger seat where Sybil slept, her head lolled to one side and mouth partially open in soft breathing. She looked peaceful, and so very beautiful in the night shadows and dim starlight. Listening to her heartbeat, he thought of her body warming his cool one as they lay in bed, arms wrapped around each other in contentment. He longed to put this Umaq chaos behind them, to enjoy life while not having to sleep with one eye open in case a demon smashed through the bedroom door.

Marcelo looked into the rearview mirror at the shadowy form of Johann in the backseat. The werewolf sat awake, staring off through the window and lost in his own thoughts. Their friendship over the decades had been full of understanding and kinship as supernatural beings. Different lives and paths had kept the two apart, but Marcelo had the utmost respect and gratitude for Johann. The werewolf could have elected to stay with Dom and take care of the bed and breakfast. Instead, he chose to accompany a distant friend for the greater good and leave behind everything he loved.

Around midnight, Marcelo crossed over to US-199 south in Josephine County and coasted into the city of Cave Junction. He drove past Watkins Street and pulled into the Holiday Motel parking lot next to Sushi Asian Cuisine. The three travelers checked into their rooms and rested until morning.

After Sybil and Johann had a quick breakfast, Marcelo donned his protective clothing against the sun. The wardrobe included a scarf, gloves, long sleeves, and a wide-brimmed hat. He resembled a mummy for the short drive to Illinois River Forks State Park. The wooded region made up part of the greater Klamath Mountains and national forest, a sprawling area of land covering millions of acres between southern Oregon and northern California.

Marcelo took the Aston Martin down a narrow service road and parked in a secluded area. Exiting the vehicle, he led the way deep into the surrounding conifers with their rich-smelling cones and needle-like leaves. Carpets of fallen needles cushioned their steps. Clusters of cones dotted the area, and a slight breeze whispered through the treetops.

"Yonder forest is a fair sight, so beautiful and serene," Sybil commented as she gazed about.

"The summer here is very pleasant," said Johann. "Dry and limited rainfall. The winter is cold with heavy snowfall, and my favorite season. I first met Salix here with snow beneath my paws and a white dusting on my coat." He smiled at Sybil. "This was back in my wilder days, before the B&B with Dom. I would tear through forests, splash through rivers, and bound up hills to blast a leaf-shaking howl at the top."

Johann stopped and took a deep breath through his nose, then released it from his mouth. He began to untie his boots. "Sorry, Marcelo, I can't help it. This mountain air is too fresh, and nature is calling. Not to use the restroom, I mean." He laughed. "I need to stretch my legs." He unfastened the belt around his jeans. "Might want to close your eyes for a second, Sybil."

"Shall you transform forthwith?" Sybil asked in an excited tone.

Marcelo noticed the animated spark in her eyes and realized Sybil had no intention of looking away as Johann threw his jeans, shirt, and underwear to the side. He grew slightly jealous, but understood this moment stood as her first time seeing a werewolf in action.

"I am," Johann replied. "I'll meet you two in Salix's grove."

Johann drew in several deep breaths. His hands opened and closed in repeated fists. He dropped to his knees and clawed the ground, then cried out, his head thrown back. Marcelo knew the shout did not signify pain, but elation. The emotional ecstasy caused by transforming equaled Marcelo's feelings when drinking blood. Pure life filled him, raw energy…a surge of spiritual and physical euphoria.

Long blond hair, the same shade from Johann's human form, sprouted all over his nude body until no skin showed. Beneath the shaggy coat his head, torso, and limbs grew with stretched bones and strong muscle. Johann's face elongated into the familiar snout of a canine. Sharp teeth formed and large ears bulged into pointed tips. Clawed paws replaced hands and feet. A bushy tail swished. Even on all fours, his head stood nearly level with Sybil's as she gaped in astonishment.

Transformation complete, the wolf stood on his rear legs and towered over the vampire and witch.

After giving a comical wink, Johann turned and bounded off in huge strides. Clods of earth, showers of pine needle, and trampled cone shrapnel flew off in all directions. The werewolf leapt high up, and hard claws grasped a tree trunk. His deep howl rolled through the forest. He then jumped to another tree and back to the ground before disappearing in the distance.

Marcelo went to collect Johann's garments and observed Sybil's fascinated expression. "Pretty cool, right?"

"'Tis a true marvel, I warrant!" she exclaimed. "There is so much wonder in the world to experience and be conversant about. Thus, it would behoove us to stop Umaq before his demons destroy it all."

Continuing on, the trees eventually thinned, and Marcelo stepped into a huge thicket of shrubs that grew from three to six feet tall. He stopped and listened to the wind rustling the small leaves and branches.

"Your other friend dwells hither, the dryad?" Sybil asked.

"Well, Salix doesn't exactly live in this place," Marcelo answered. "She *is* this place." He smiled when Sybil looked at him in bewilderment. He had refrained from giving her all the details about "little plant face", as Johann called her. Marcelo thought it would be more fun, and a better experience, for Sybil to discover Salix on her own.

"These shrubs are a species of willow called *Salix delnortensis*, or more commonly known as Del Norte willow," Marcelo began. "They are native to the Klamath Mountain region, and pockets of these shrubs can be found in northern California and in southern Oregon. Our friend Salix seems to prefer Oregon, which is why we are here."

Sybil approached a willow bush and caressed its leaves. "A long time agone, I had heard that dryads are connected to large trees, such as oak or ash. Yet I am taller than some of these plants. Surely Salix is a unique individual. Truly, I am amazed and cannot wait to have a fair sight of your friend."

Foliage rustled as something moved through the surrounding thicket. A moment later, Johann trotted into the clearing where Marcelo stood with Sybil. The large, blond werewolf appeared content as leaves, twigs, and dirt clung all over his shaggy form. A powerful shake of his body sent debris scattering. He then sat on his haunches and nodded toward a knot of bushes as the wind picked up.

Marcelo felt the sudden breeze flow through the area. Branches rattled, leaves danced, and discarded pine needles skittered across the ground. However, this was no common gust as words formed in the natural movement and noise around him. Each bent leaf or swaying branch signified a method of communication by Salix. Clattering grit as it rolled, a falling cone when it hit the ground, even the flap of a bird's wing indicated thoughts and emotions. The dryad called out, pleased at seeing her friends.

"I can hear her," Sybil whispered in awe. She looked at Marcelo, tears in her eyes. "Her language is so very beautiful, I warrant. Salix is…everywhere and everything in yonder place!"

Marcelo wasn't surprised that she could hear the dryad. His beloved witch had a lifetime of experience calling on nature spirits and communicating with deities during various spells and rituals. Years spent in forests, meadows, caves, and other areas around nature while performing magic placed her in tune with most forms of the mystical and divine.

It had taken Marcelo and Johann months to learn Salix's language. Marcelo had spent several hours a day listening to the wind and studying nature's movement in response. At first, only one or two words could be discerned. After time and patience, whole sentences and the emotions behind them emerged. The sensation of communicating with the dryad had astonished him, just as Sybil experienced it now.

"My name is Sybil," she said to the willow shrubs. "Of a truth, 'tis an honor and delight to meet you, Salix." Smiling, she wiped her eyes.

Johann whined, sniffed, and uttered low growls as he spoke with Salix. The werewolf pawed the ground, then nudged one of the shrubs. He finally stood at full height, his hairy arms crossed in impatience.

"He wants her to come out now, but Salix is a bit shy," Marcelo told Sybil. "You are right about her being everywhere and everything in this place. The Del Norte willow are clones created from one individual bush. Her spirit lies in all of them, but it doesn't stop just there. Salix's consciousness can reside in any *delnortensis* thicket, even ones south of the state border in California hundreds of miles away."

Sybil shook her head as wonder lit her gaze. "I can truly only imagine the profound knowledge she conceives. Yonder mountains and forests are ancient. Thus, it would be remarkable to learn from her." She glanced around. "My heart wishes for Salix to come forth for an appropriate greeting."

Two squirrels darted between the bushes and up a tree. The scurry of paws across the turf and up the bark came to Marcelo as the dryad's translated words: *I am ready*.

A knot of bare branches sprouted from the ground. The top part of a head followed, the branches protruding from the scalp like wiry hair. Halting just above ground level, brilliant emerald eyes darted between Marcelo and the others. Long lashes blinked away remnants of soil that trickled down Salix's forehead.

Marcelo couldn't help but smile. "There's no one else here, Salix. Join us now so we can all hug you properly."

The head fully emerged sporting a thin nose and no mouth. A patch of cherry-colored bark covered her right temple, and velvety moss coated her left cheek. Shoulders, torso, and arms pushed forth as soil, bits of cone, and pine needles cascaded to the ground. Her legs and feet appeared last while she shook each foot to clear them of dirt. Over skin the color of a green olive, random patches of bark, moss, or bunches of leaves grew.

Salix stood around four feet tall, slim and resembling a child. But her vivid emerald eyes revealed a tale of longevity and ancient wisdom. She had dwelled in the land ages before humans appeared. Salix's roots penetrated the soil and connected her to nature everywhere. She spoke to the earth's heart and lived in its pulse—knowing, learning, and evolving with changes throughout time.

Johann bent down to lick Salix's arms and legs in a fervid greeting. The dryad lacked a mouth, but a physical smile proved unnecessary for her to express joy. Her eyes sparkled in delight as she threw her arms around the werewolf's neck. A flock of birds burst forth from a shrub. Feathers drifted down, pure laughter as Marcelo recognized the emotional translation.

After the embrace, Sybil approached and gently grasped Salix's bark and leaf-covered hands. "My friendship and service are yours, dear dryad. Truly, you are beautiful beyond words."

Salix nuzzled her velvet-covered cheek against one of Sybil's hands, the soft rasp a communication. *I look forward to this friendship, Spell Weaver. I am satisfied.*

Stepping forward, Marcelo lowered to one knee and took Salix into his arms. He inhaled the dryad's fresh scent of rich, moist earth and dew-speckled leaves. The smell of blossoming flowers and sharp pine also wafted from her like perfume. He ran the backs of his fingers across a velvety patch of moss on her upper arm.

"And I'm a terrible friend," he said softly. "I should have visited you more often."

The breeze skittered fallen leaves across the ground as Salix spoke. *You are here now, Marcelo. That is all that matters. I am happy.*

"As am I, which is why I feel guilty for asking you to come with me toward danger," Marcelo said as he stood. "I'm certain you're aware of the rise in demonic activity in our world and of the celestial tremor as even the lunar deities are at odds."

I am cognizant of the demon master and of the fractured moon. Two cones fell from trees surrounding the thicket as Salix spoke. *The natural order is growing more unbalanced. The earth weeps. I am sad.*

"We will need your help," Marcelo continued. "Umaq and Cessani are very powerful. You know what will happen if they succeed in casting down the sun god."

A strong gust shook the surrounding treetops and branches creaked. *Roots groan in pain deep inside the earth. The scent on the wind turns sour. Mystical barriers crack under strain. I will travel with you. I am worried.*

Marcelo gave a solemn nod, then exchanged glances with everyone as mixed emotions battered him. Satisfaction over having a motivated, gifted team filled him with determination. Yet dread buried itself deep in his gut, a creeping anxiety over his friends' wellbeing. Demons, witches, and deities…how dangerous would the upcoming battle be? Could he protect everyone? If something happened to Sybil—

Marcelo broke off the thought. Hesitation and worry proved contagious. He needed to remain strong and radiate some confidence. Together, his team would succeed to rid the world of darkness.

He crossed his arms. "So it's settled, and time is short." He looked at Sybil. "Our resident witch has a plan to get us to Machu Picchu. Let's work out the details, and rest before we leave tonight."

Johann lifted Salix and placed the petite dryad on his furry shoulders. Marcelo took Sybil's hand and squeezed it with affection. The group headed back through the forest and one step closer to a showdown against Umaq.

Chapter Six

A Hell of a Ride

In the car during the three-hour drive to Crater Lake, Sybil explained her plan to the others. Back in Nevada City before leaving for Cave Junction, she had performed research on her tome of technology—her smartphone—to familiarize herself with the Oregon territory. Looking for something very specific, she discovered Wizard Island in Crater Lake, the key for taking Umaq and Cessani by surprise.

"Ley line travel," Johann commented from the rear seat behind Marcelo. Back in human form, his blond hair no longer draped in a ponytail. Instead, loose strands hung past his shoulders.

Gazing at him from the front passenger seat, Sybil studied his dark, pensive eyes and rather grim expression while waiting for a response to her plan. Traveling by ley line into the heart of Machu Picchu contained risks, and she wasn't certain she could even open a gate. But if successful, the action provided the element of surprise and a preemptive strike.

Johann's brooding face finally broke into a grin. "It will be a hell of a ride. I can't wait to rip some demon heads off before they know it."

Twisting a bit further in the seat, Sybil glanced at Salix next to Johann. The quiet dryad ran a finger across a leafy patch on her thigh, the rustling foliage portraying her words. *A hell of a ride. I am eager.*

Smiling at them both, Sybil turned back around and patted Marcelo on the knee as he drove. He gave her a reassuring wink, and she relaxed in the seat. Coasting on Crater Lake Highway northeast of Sams Valley, a star-filled summer sky stretched overhead.

Leaving from Oregon at night and arriving in Machu Picchu while it remained dark proved essential. Marcelo would be incapable of fighting during the day. If exposed to the sun, the light would scald and weaken him. As for Johann, his natural and more powerful transformation cycle occurred at night. The werewolf required darkness to function at his best.

A long, winding road skirting the edge of Crater Lake took them to Watchman Peak Trail on the western rim. Marcelo pulled off the highway and parked in the dirt. Johann grabbed a large box from the trunk, an inflatable raft they had purchased in Cave Junction. Carrying a flashlight, Sybil moved to the edge of the massive crater and carefully scampered down the steep, sandy slope that led to the lake.

She approached the water and thought how wonderful it would be to visit this national park with Marcelo during a time of peace. While in the bed and breakfast, she had imagined traveling on a vacation, and Crater Lake could have been one of their destinations. She recalled what her Oregon research stated about this location, as the pictures and history fascinated her.

Crater Lake is a remnant of a destroyed volcano called Mount Mazama, which exploded between six and eight thousand years ago. No streams flow into the crater; precipitation fills the bottom to form the blue lake, yet eventually the water evaporates or disappears from seepage. When the crater is full after snow and rainfall, the lake becomes the deepest in the United States.

On the shore, Johann opened the box and used the battery-operated pump to fill the large raft with air. Sybil waded knee-deep into the lake and climbed aboard with the others. Marcelo grabbed the plastic oars and rowed the quarter mile across Skell Channel to Wizard Island.

Sybil had also read that Wizard Island was a volcanic cinder cone, a protrusion of land caused by secondary explosions following the original eruption of Mount Mazama. A dormant volcanic crater capped a small mountain centered on the island—the gateway into a ley line. Ironically, the small crater was named "Witches Cauldron" by William Gladstone Steel, who also named the island.

Sybil splashed back into the cold water and helped pull the raft onto the western shore of the island. Clicking on her light, the beam illuminated scant trees and stony soil. Marching along, the group began the three quarters of a mile hike to the top of the mini volcano.

Salix appeared at Sybil's side. The small dryad had no trouble keeping pace with everyone's longer strides. Salix's bark-crusted feet crunched over gravel and kicked at loose stones. Sybil listened to the sounds, and through them, the dryad communicated in her unique language.

You must have a grand story behind you, Spell Weaver. You are proficient in speaking to faerie and other spirits of the tree. It is a pleasure to know you. I am impressed.

"And my heart is very thrilled to have met you," Sybil responded. "But of a truth, you would not be so impressed by the evil I had done weeks agone. Honesty between friends is vital. I shall tell you all about my life when this is over, I warrant."

Salix ran a hand through the dozens of small branches sprouting from her head, the wooden clatter her response. *Marcelo trusts you and that makes me feel the same, although I do not know your history. But the love in his eyes for you, and in yours for him, is evident. I am glad.*

"He hath saved me in many ways. Hitherto, I am fortunate to have him in my life." Sybil glanced at the dryad. "I conceive some of the twigs on your head are bare and brittle. Others are more supple and velvety or wooly. Might that have to do with the growth cycle of yonder Del Norte willow?"

A breeze rattled the leaves on Salix's body, and she spoke. *Yes, you are very observant. The older branches lack any covering and are fragile. The younger shoots wear their coats of velvet with pride. I have no age, Sybil. Like flowers in the passing of seasons, I am always growing...and dying. I am ordinary.*

"Truly, I do not know if I ought to find that somber or accept it as nature's beautiful miracle." Sybil smiled, then reached out and squeezed Salix's shoulder. "You are certainly not ordinary, my dear friend."

The dryad reached up and broke off one of the younger twigs from her head. She then held it out to Sybil. *Mystical properties thrive in the wood. Opening the gate to a ley line is difficult, and the branch may aid your spell weaving. I am certain.*

Sybil's mouth opened in awe as she accepted the remarkable gift. A velvety green coat wrapped half the stick, its length about six inches and the width of a pencil. The magic inside the wood hummed and tingled her fingertips. She had owned dozens of enchanted talismans and spell books, but never anything so potent as a fragment of dryad's essence.

"Thank you, Salix. I am in your debt." Sybil studied the branch and shook her head. "This is truly very special, and I shall cherish it."

Winded after a steep climb up the large hill, Sybil reached the top alongside the others and stood on the edge of Witches Cauldron, the mouth of the long dormant cinder cone. From the highest point on Wizard Island, a gorgeous view of night presented all around. The normal blue hue of surrounding Crater Lake shone black beneath the darkened sky. Twinkling light from the countless stars and crescent moon floated on the water's surface. Around the lake, the encircling edges of the crater rose upwards like a bowl.

"It's spectacular up here," Marcelo commented. "I could look at this for hours."

"So could I, but we don't have much time," said Johann. "Peru is two hours ahead of us. It's after ten here, so just past midnight in Machu Picchu. How long will the ley line ride be, Sybil?"

"Ley lines are nearly as good as portals," she answered. "We ought to arrive almost instantly, I warrant. Yet of a truth, the traveling itself shall feel like it takes much longer. Or…so I have heard."

"You've heard?" Johann asked. "This is your first time doing this sort of thing?"

Sybil gave him a slow nod.

Johann widened his eyes and scratched the top of his head. "I don't remember you admitting that when explaining the plan in the car."

Feeling everyone's eyes on her, Sybil looked down into the darkened mouth of the cauldron. She had heard a saying on the TV, something she had asked Marcelo to explain. The phrase now flashed in her mind. Had she *bitten off more than she could chew*? Doubt started to creep beneath her skin. She took a deep breath and tried to push the uncertainty away.

"This is the best way to get inside Umaq's fortress," Marcelo explained. "Even the military, with all their training and firepower, haven't been able to penetrate the defenses. There's no way to sneak past a horde of demons or fight our way through them. The ley line will place us right inside." His arm wrapped Sybil in a supportive embrace. "You'll do great, love. Just tell us what you need."

Marcelo's hug and inspiring words restored some of Sybil's confidence; any lingering hesitation she ignored. "Everyone remaineth hither at the edge while I go down yonder. It shall take a few moments to prepare the spell to open the gate. Fear not, I shall call you when it is safe."

Marcelo kissed her mouth. "You're the boss. We'll wait right here."

Johann blew out a breath and appeared uneasy. After a moment, he smiled and pumped a fist. "You got this, most powerful witch on the planet."

Salix gestured to the branch in Sybil's hand, then her foot scraped the rocky earth to communicate. *Plant the wood in the ground, and focus your energies there. I am hopeful.*

Sybil nodded at her friends. "I shall go forth and begin."

She carefully stepped down the rocky slope and into the heart of the Witches Cauldron. Ages ago, the top of the cinder cone had been filled with soil and stone. Now, the hollow depression receded a couple hundred feet deep. In the beam of her flashlight, a few bushes and two or three trees dotted the area. Locating the very bottom of the bowl, she glanced back the way she came and saw the glint of someone's flashlight on the rim above.

Sybil inserted the dryad's short branch into the ground. A low hum began and vibrated the surrounding soil. Buried beneath her feet, the entrance to a ley line pulsed like an artery. Throughout the world, ley lines connected numerous ancient structures and prominent landmarks. The rare lines consisted of powerful earth energies, mystical rivers flowing across the planet. The concentrated points stood in places such as Stonehenge, the Egyptian pyramids, and Machu Picchu. Throughout history, these ley line areas had become centers for astronomy, religion, societal development, nature studies, and worship.

But for travel? Sybil had heard rumors and perhaps read a passage or two in old dusty books. Speculation did not represent qualification for opening a ley line gate. If an error occurred, she might hurt someone, or the group could become lost inside the subterranean flows.

Yet renewed faith suddenly burned inside her. Even with risks, she desired to tear open the earth and journey on its spiritual rivers. And why not? She may lack the experience, but the power to do the impossible throbbed within her mind and body.

Despite the unforgivable acts Umaq had done to her, he had roused untapped magical potential inside her after she awoke from her three-hundred-year slumber. Immense spiritual energies and exhilarating powers she never imagined having before exploded to life. Teleporting short distances represented one of them she had performed in Boston for the first time. Manipulation of the elements for attack and protection were other powerful spells, similar to the ones used to destroy the mighty demon Nala'thelx. Why possess these marvelous abilities and not use them?

Sybil gazed up into the black, star-speckled sky. The infinite celestial bodies motivated her to surpass her limits. "I can do this, I warrant. I *need* to do this."

She stared at the branch protruding from the ground. Using Salix's advice, she set her flashlight aside and focused her energy on the wood. Spreading her arms, she tensed her muscles and *pushed* her spiritual power outwards. Illuminated white tendrils wafted from her body like smoke. The places on her flesh where the tendrils rose burned as if touched by a hot poker. She suppressed a scream, then grit her teeth as tears streamed down her cheeks.

The glowing spiritual mist drifted to the ground and swirled around Sybil's feet. Intense pain amplified her voice as she shouted the spell. "*Up high, down low, and lost in-between. From here, to there, a distant mirage's sheen. As a compass spins and direction hides in fate, I call upon the earth spirits…OPEN THE GATE!"*

The underground hum grew louder. The ground trembled, and Sybil nearly lost her balance. Rocks from the surrounding slope tumbled into the bottom of Witches Cauldron. Bushes and trees shook. She thought she heard Marcelo's voice call her name over the commotion.

The ground began to crack. Sybil grabbed the branch just as the tear widened to swallow the wood. A large mouth formed, teal-colored light blasting into the sky. The shaking earth knocked her down as she ran to a safe distance. A moment later, strong arms lifted Sybil to her feet.

"Are you all right?" Marcelo asked in a shout over the loud buzz. Johann and Salix had also climbed down the slope to gape at the open ley line.

"We all need to jump inside forthwith," Sybil managed to say, out of breath. "The gate shall not remaineth open for long."

Marcelo signaled to the others and cupped his hands around his mouth. "Let's go in!"

Johann picked up Salix, a protective father scooping up a child. "See you inside," he hollered, then leapt in.

Sybil grasped Marcelo's hand, and together, they dropped into the roaring light.

Chapter Seven

Moon Madness

Grace left her home and drove the Prius north on Highway 1A further into Salem. For the past twenty minutes, she had turned on random streets, doubled back, stopped for a short while, then continued in haphazard directions. She hoped the darkness of night and her erratic driving patterns would shake off any pursuers. She had organized an emergency meeting with her coven in the Forest River Conservation Area, and it became essential she arrive unnoticed by the enemy.

She exited on Grant Road, then performed a U-turn. Heading back, she stopped before pulling back onto the highway and glanced into the rearview mirror. A set of headlights followed her. Did the vehicle pose a danger, or just someone passing through?

Grace shrieked when something pounded the hood of her car. Frozen, she stared through the windshield in horror. She had been too focused on the scene behind her and failed to notice the red-robed zombie in the road. One of Nastasiya's animated corpses swayed before the bumper. Worms wriggled and fell from holes in its ruined face. The creature raised its fists and slammed them on the hood again.

Grace's eyes flicked to the rearview mirror in panic.

The headlights drew closer. She held the steering

wheel in an iron grip and uttered a spell focused on the taillights of her car. *"Quite right beautiful night, make these lights shine so bright!"*

A giant flash of red pierced the darkness behind her. The powerful burst of light would blind any observers for several seconds—hopefully enough time for her car to disappear. Grace mashed the pedal and plowed into the zombie. The undead monster rolled over the hood and up the windshield, then dropped onto the road as she sped away.

Grace maneuvered the vehicle into a hard left on the highway. She then threw the car into an immediate right onto Pickman Road and raced down the narrow treelined street. Well into the forest, she turned left on Arnold Drive and stopped the car in a cul-de-sac, her heart pounding.

Several minutes ticked by in silence. Just when she thought the danger had passed, a pickup truck turned onto the street and headed straight for her. Her heart raced again—then slowed as she recognized the blue Toyota. The truck pulled up beside her car and the passenger window lowered, the cab light on. The young couple inside peered anxiously at Grace.

"Ben, Elisa, I'm so glad you made it safely," Grace said in relief, hoping they hadn't encountered any trouble on the way. "Let's wait for the others. If no one else can make it, we'll have to perform the ritual on our own."

Less than ten minutes later, she recognized a silver minivan pulling into the street and parking behind her. Several members of her coven emerged from the packed vehicle. Ben and Elisa climbed out of their truck, and Grace met everyone in the street for hugs.

"Is everyone all right?" she asked. "I'm so happy to see all of you! Cessani's goons are still spying on us, but it looks like we did our part to arrive here unnoticed. There's not much time. Let's hurry into the forest and get this over with. I have a bone to pick with the Mother and the Crone."

Flashlight in hand and backpack secure, Grace led her coven deep into the forested Conservation Area. She felt confident no unwanted eyes peered or outsiders followed, but each unexpected step on a noisy twig or leaf made her skin crawl in gooseflesh.

She marched the coven toward the Forest River and halted when they reached a clearing along its marshy banks. The darkened, moist, and insect-filled environment failed to provide much comfort. However, the seclusion and the old tree spirits near the water offered the best location for performing a ritual to send Grace to the moon goddesses.

The coven formed a circle and knelt on the damp ground. Each member lit a white candle and set it before them. From the backpack, Grace removed three pewter chalices and filled two from the small river. After setting the chalices in the middle of the circle, she added two candles, a red and a black. Grace ignited the two candles, then added a white one that remained dark. The empty goblet and the unlit candle represented the Maiden's departure from the trio of moon deities. A pile of fresh grapes and a block of cheese came next—an offering for the tree spirits in gratitude for their mystical energy used during the rite. Lastly, the Three of Cups from the Tarot deck represented the final piece as it lay next to the other items.

Grace returned to her place in the circle. She began an incantation, and the coven followed her lead.

"Goddess of night, deity of moon. The three are now two, please hear our cry soon. The Maiden is lost, and the moon sheds its glow. Dear Mother and Crone, there is something we must know. Goddess of night, deity of moon..."

The chant repeated several more times. A chill washed over Grace, and she stood to walk to the center. Turning around, she saw her body still kneeling at the circle's edge, eyes closed and mouth moving with the spell. She felt calm, understanding the enchantment had taken effect. Her essence now moved free. In this state, she could see glowing tree spirits in the form of monkeys perched in the branches. Others fashioned after squirrels ran playfully along the riverbank. Three spirits shaped like racoons gnawed on the grapes and cheese.

Grace looked into the night sky, where three giant moons filled the darkness: a waxing crescent, full sphere, and a waning moon. The Maiden's waxing crescent suddenly shattered in a thousand brilliant shards that fell to the earth. A loon cried in the distance and a wolf howled. A fierce wind tore through the circle. Grace shouted in surprise as her disembodied form lifted from the ground and sailed toward the remaining moons.

She glanced back over her shoulder and saw the forest growing smaller. Soon the features of Salem became lost in hundreds of distant twinkling lights. Her speed accelerated. The full moon increased in size and brightness as Grace zoomed toward it. Very close now, the moon filled her entire vision, and she recognized giant craters, dusty valleys, and a disquieting void.

Slowing, she touched down on the moon's surface and felt like an astronaut in those old photos of the Apollo missions. Even the blue, white, and brown marble of the Earth showed in the distance among the blackness of space.

"You're not really standing on the moon," a voice suddenly spoke.

Grace turned and saw a middle-aged woman wearing an astronaut suit, but no helmet. Long white hair cascaded over the shoulders and down the back of the bulky suit. A hint of amusement showed in cobalt eyes as the Mother winked.

"Mother Goddess," Grace said, inclining her head to the deity. "What is this place?"

"These images and surroundings were created by your mind," the Mother replied. "I'm going along with it because I find it interesting. But the moon and the Earth don't exist here. We're not really anywhere."

Another voice spoke out from behind Grace. "Where we are doesn't matter. The question is *why*." Squeezed into an astronaut suit, the old Crone approached and joined the others. Short, white hair cropped at chin level surrounded a wrinkled face. Her azure eyes matched the Mother's, but instead of amusement, irritation swam in her expression.

"I would like to talk about the Maiden," Grace began. "She—"

"Yes, yes, we are quite aware of what she has done," the Crone interrupted. "The foolish, headstrong girl abandoned the Triple Moon Goddess notion and is freelancing around witches. She is also helping that maniac, Umaq, bring more demons into the world to exterminate a sun god."

"And you have done nothing," Grace dared to say.

Nervous, it took all her internal strength and will to speak so boldly to the goddesses. If she had been in her physical body, she'd tremble as sweat moistened her palms. However, she hadn't endured evil witches, zombies, car chases, and fearing for life to back down now. This opportunity with the deities presented her only chance to seek divine assistance.

The Crone's crumpled expression flared a shade of red as she waddled closer to Grace. Her awkward movements in the large white suit made her resemble an Apollo astronaut even more.

"Insolent witch!" the deity said. "If you invoked us only to—"

"Let's hear what she has to say," the Mother stepped in. "I imagine Grace went through a lot of trouble to be here."

"Thank you, Mother," Grace replied, somewhat relieved. She had expected to be thrown down to the forest right away. At least she had a chance to speak, but she still might be tossed back afterwards with nothing resolved.

"Sybil and Marcelo are attempting to stop Umaq from destroying the sun god, but they're at a major disadvantage and I fear for their wellbeing," Grace began. "Led by the Maiden, Cessani is another dangerous obstacle to my friends' success. Even my coven in Salem is not safe with powerful witches and necromancy at work in the streets. Mama Quilla has chosen the side of darkness as well. Is there nothing the Mother and Crone can do to assist? I apologize for being forward, but so much has happened and it seems the both of you have remained silent on the matter."

"We have," the Mother said matter-of-factly. "For a number of reasons. It's true the Maiden can be a brat on occasion. When she stomps her foot and believes she knows everything, only failure and humility will reel her in. Sometimes it's best to let her experience that on her own without pointless arguing or interference. When her silly plan and little adventure backfire, she'll return with her head hung low."

"Or she may get bored of her new endeavor and decide to come home anyway," the Crone added. "Fickle is the best way to describe her."

"Those are your reasons for being inactive?" Grace asked in disbelief. "You can't guarantee that Umaq and Cessani will fail, or that the Maiden will simply lose interest. People are in real danger and your hands-off approach is only worsening the situation. My friends are placing their lives at risk. We cannot let evil win."

"Who are you to decide what is malevolent?" the Crone asked. "We are cognizant of your witch friend, the young girl Sybil. Not too long ago she represented the epitome of evil. What is considered wrong in your eyes may not be so for the Mother and I."

"The Crone is right," the Mother said. "Natural balances may shift with the fall of a sun god, but not enough to endanger us as moon deities. In fact, the greater lunar energy will provide some benefit. Our followers are increasing as more witches come forth and choose sides in this conflict."

"And the sides do not matter," the Crone added before Grace could get a word out. "Whether it's your coven or Cessani's, both groups of witches worship the Maiden, Mother, and Crone to use in their rituals and spell casting. The Triple Moon Goddess itself may no longer be valid, but individually, we still function to provide guidance, wisdom, and mystical power to those who adore and respect us."

"Even to you, Grace," the Mother finished.

Back in the forest, Grace's kneeling body reacted with a deep, frustrated sigh. Here in her spirit form, she maintained her composure, although anger swelled inside. She wanted to grab the deities by their bulky suits and shake sense into them. Why did they act so nonchalant? Did they not care about the wellbeing of mortals, only being worshipped?

"Well, I am left entirely disappointed," Grace stated. "I expected more from the lunar goddesses as leaders and symbols of inspiration and hope. You were right about Sybil. She did terrible things to people, but in the end, she at least chose a side and now fights for the greater good. Witches may still idolize you, but the Maiden has made a complete mockery of the Triple Moon Goddess—your very essence and meaning for existence. The trio is who you are. Since the beginning of time, it's what thousands of generations have known you as. The concept is legendary, and your true strength and purpose lies in the Three. That, Goddesses, is what is natural and should be."

"We appreciate the motivational speech, but this is a matter for deities," the Crone remarked. She waved her hand, and an old 70s model of a lunar rover appeared. She settled into the passenger seat and pointed to the Mother. "You drive. Might as well take advantage of the scenery while we're here."

The Mother studied Grace with a curious expression. She then gestured to the distant marble of the Earth, and the globe zoomed in similar to searching a location on Google Maps. The deity centered the picture on Salem. Grace spotted the forest her body knelt in and the surrounding streets and highways.

Red dots appeared in various locations across the city and in several neighborhoods. "These sites are where Cessani's witches and their new undead pets are stationed while they spy on you and your coven," the Mother explained. She approached Grace and laid a gloved hand on her shoulder. "The Crone and I may be neutral on the subject of the Maiden, but please accept this information as a sign that we are not so insensible."

Grace bowed her head. "I appreciate the helpful tip on my enemy's whereabouts and will use this to my advantage." She offered the goddesses a half-hearted smile. "I'm ready to return now. Thank you both for your time and for hearing me out."

The Mother headed for the rover and settled behind the wheel. "Farewell, Grace," she called. "Know that our blessings go with you."

A force suddenly propelled Grace backwards. She reversed course from the moon and watched it shrink while her spirit flew back to the forest. Soon she stood in the middle of the circle, her beloved coven continuing the ritual until her return. She stepped toward her body and knelt in its same position to complete the union.

Grace opened her eyes. She stood in a wince, rubbing her sore knees and lower back. At middle-age, the spry days of leaping to her feet after spell casting were long past. One by one, the coven broke the circle to rise and gaze at her in anticipation of good news. Hope for celestial assistance had depended on this secret—and dangerous—ritual. Each member had risked harm to arrive safely. Like Grace, her friends' lives had been turned upside down by demons and malicious witches. They felt hunted and nervous about being spied upon when merely going to the grocery store.

Grace had to break their hearts. She had failed to provide hope and protection. The moon goddesses showed little interest in her affairs and those of the world. She looked at each of her friends, her grave expression and barest shake of her head enough to portray the message of ruined hope. As if to emphasize the rejection, in the center of the circle she poured out river water from the chalices representing the Mother and the Crone. She then snuffed out the red and black candles. Any optimism dried with the spilled water. Confidence vanished in the dissipating candle smoke.

The coven watched in silent grief, but anger and frustration at their predicament swelled inside Grace. She threw the coven a sharp glare and loudly clapped her hands twice. "Enough! No time for sorrow or giving up. The deities may have turned their backs on us, but the Mother left me with some valuable information on our enemy. I want to go on the offensive, my friends. I'm tired of running, hiding, and fearing for my life. But I refuse to place any of you in additional danger. If you do not wish to participate in my plan, then you have my blessing."

"We are with you, Grace," Ben said as Elisa added an enthusiastic nod.

The rest of the coven did not hesitate to join with calls of agreement and support. The group drew together and draped arms around each other like a celebrating baseball team, Grace smiling at the center. Their courage, passion, and determination filled her with adoration as tears blurred her vision.

"Then it's time to take back the streets!" she shouted to the sky.

Chapter Eight

Scorched Plans

Hefting a backpack over a shoulder, Umaq grabbed a shovel and headed out from his stone hovel into the daylight. He used a hand to block the sun's glare and inspected the sky for military aircraft, but didn't spot a single one. The noise of gunfire and explosions had also remained silent since yesterday. The lack of battle activity had presented him the best night of sleep since arriving at Machu Picchu. He felt rested and in much better spirits.

Good progress had been made toward opening the portal in the Temple of the Three Windows. Cessani's witches had done their part to stir the mountain's dormant spiritual energy. Through endless hours of spell preparation and chants, Umaq had used the renewed mystical essence to strengthen the portal in the Uku-Pacha window. He only needed a little more time to activate the gateway to the netherworld. Once he achieved completion, a stronger demon army would pour through to aid in Inti's destruction.

With some extra time available, Umaq woke this morning having a specific task in mind, something he anticipated even before traveling to Peru. He adjusted the backpack on his shoulders and strolled down a stone path in the residential district of the rebuilt ruins. Just ahead, Cessani came into view with a small group of witches behind her. Not wanting any distractions, Umaq attempted to turn on a different path, but Cessani spotted him and waved him over.

White streaks of age blended amongst the dark strands cascading from Cessani's head. Attached to the left shoulder of her red robe, a silver pin shaped like a waxing moon glinted in the sun. The old witch's dark brown eyes glanced at the shovel in Umaq's hand as he approached.

"Going off to assist in fortifying the walls?" she asked. "You have demons for that."

"Where I'm going is none of your business," he replied. He studied the knot of men and women gathered on the path. Each of them wore the same silver pin as Cessani. "New arrivals?"

"Yes, and a wonderful addition to our ranks," she said. "These are skilled *brujas* and *chamáns* from all around South America. As natives to the continent, they are well connected to the mystical energies here. In the short time since arriving, they've already boosted the magic necessary for your portal. You should thank them."

Umaq had noticed the increase in power from the mountain, but he wasn't much for pleasantries. He offered a curt nod to the group.

"Welcome to Machu Picchu, and…thanks," he grumbled. "I have work to do." He stepped around the crowd and continued on.

Umaq later approached a crumbling, untouched hovel distanced from the rest of the residential area. The thatch roof had collapsed long ago, and many of the granite blocks in the walls had shifted. He had ordered the worker demons not to go near this place—his ancient home from nearly five hundred years ago.

A volatile mixture of nostalgia and repulsion assaulted Umaq as he stepped through the entryway. A flood of both enjoyable and rage-filled memories dizzied him, a prior era of triumphs and disaster. As a youth, he had loved life and respected the community of his fellow Inca. As an adult priest, ingratitude from his people and betrayal by deities had poisoned him. But after centuries, the antidote had arrived. Umaq finally stood ready to destroy Inti and eradicate his own past failures.

One such failure lay buried beneath the ritual chamber of his old home. He found the room barren as any past archeologists had cleaned out the pottery, parchment, or tools he might have left lying around. Weeds grew over most of the dirt floor. With no roof, sunlight shone on the ruins of a stone fire pit. Umaq shrugged out of the backpack and set it on the ground. He drove the shovel into the soil and began to dig.

The ritual chamber had been the center of his twisted experiments. Summoning demons, casting dark magic, and research into necromancy were some of the works he performed. One of his greatest achievements had been opening a minor portal into the demon realm. An army of lesser demons, and the stronger and more intelligent Nala'thelx, had streamed out into the world. Many of those easily manipulated creatures remained at his side to rebuild the citadel and fight off mortals.

While useful, the minor portal crafted in the fire pit did not offer enough power to summon greater demons. Umaq required some major muscle to take down the sun god, and the Uku-Pacha window in the

Temple of the Three Windows provided the answer. Through that portal lay the true door to the deep nether, and powerful monstrosities would soon come forth under his command.

Dirt flew as Umaq continued to unearth his past. Sweat trickled into his eyes and moistened his shirt. He paused to drink from a canteen in the backpack and splash water over his face. He eventually cast the shovel aside and used his hands to carefully remove a demon's bones from the cool soil.

The complete skeleton of a monster had lain buried here for centuries. Not just any creature, but the very demon whose spirit now resided inside Marcelo. When Umaq had apprehended the young Spanish Conquistador, the intent had been to kill the teen and replace his soul with the demon's. That part of the trial succeeded; however, the resurrected Marcelo failed to submit to the spells of control. As a master demon summoner, Umaq surmised he had the ability to command the malevolent spirit while hosted by an empty human vessel. Unexpected and infuriating, Marcelo had retained his memories, emotions, and human consciousness while the monster's essence raged inside him.

Umaq had labeled the project a fiasco. The only thing he accomplished was producing a secondhand vampire, a lost creature who couldn't even identify with the true species of undead vampires that consisted of former humans lacking a soul. To worsen matters—and what really fueled his hatred of the situation—he had failed to control Marcelo for a second time in the Wyman Woods near Salem. Sybil had contributed to Umaq's letdown during that incident, and he vowed to remedy the situation by destroying them both after dealing with Inti.

The long dead demon buried in the ground still had a part to play. Umaq cleaned the bones and placed the smaller ones inside the backpack. He rolled the longer, bigger bones inside cloth and tied the collection into a large bundle. The task finished, he gathered everything and headed for the Temple of the Three Windows.

Once there, he placed the bones inside a heavy wooden coffer and locked it. While he sat on the lid and drank from the canteen, the temperature in the area suddenly increased. Outside, the midday light grew brighter and the ground rumbled. Demonic howls and human shouts rose from the surrounding courtyard in a frantic crescendo. Umaq bolted to his feet. Had the military launched a surprise attack?

He ran outside into the Sacred Plaza and stopped dead. A gasp of disbelief and terror seized his throat. Nearly too bright to observe, a ball of light the size of a house hovered over the Central Plaza, a wide strip of grass that ran the length of Machu Picchu and divided the city.

Inti the sun god had manifested!

But how? The old god had been dormant for centuries. Umaq's plan consisted of summoning Inti after the portal had been opened and his demon army stood ready. The portal remained closed due to a shortage of spiritual power, and he needed more time. Now the sun god burned overhead…and Umaq had no forces prepared. A handful of Cessani's witches stood frozen in fear. The worker demons barked, howled, and ran wild all over the grounds.

"Umaq, The Betrayer!" Inti's voice commanded from the radiant sphere as it descended into the green belt. The grass smoked and blackened as the ball rested on the ground. "Did you believe I could be beckoned at will? Am I subservient to a mortal? The mountain woke me. I sensed the mystical energies rising to the heavens after your foolish witches activated the earth. Your imprudent actions are over. Come forth, Betrayer, and kneel before me!"

"So much for fighting him at night," Cessani said, out of breath as she reached Umaq's side on the stone path. "The darkness would have made him weaker and the moon goddesses stronger. We have no choice now."

"Delay him, Cessani," Umaq said as his heart raced. "Do whatever you can. I'll send all the lesser demons at him as well. I must somehow activate the portal or die trying."

"Well, I certainly don't plan on dying," Cessani replied. Fear danced in her dark eyes as she rubbed her hands together in unease. "The moon goddesses and I will give the sun deity a run for his money. Now go and tear that portal off its hinges before it's too late!"

With a shouted command, Umaq regained control of the frenzied demon horde and launched the growling mass toward Inti. Four-legged, upright, and winged creatures swarmed at the sun god barring teeth and claws. Sizzling sunbeams exploded from the hovering ball and incinerated random demons. Umaq knew these monsters couldn't do much against the sun god, but he hoped they would provide enough of a distraction for Cessani and her coven to buy more time.

Umaq raced into the Temple of the Three Windows. He glared at the Uku-Pacha window, a dozen thoughts spinning. How could he access the portal while having an insufficient amount of energy? The answer might be in his tomes—no time for that. What ancient chants for opening or summoning did he know? Not enough…too many…none that would help.

No time to think—only act. Umaq unlocked the wooden coffer and threw back the lid. Careful with the bones, he rummaged through the other contents and pulled out a jar of granulated puma blood. He added a lightning-charged gem set in a medallion, a ceramic box filled with faerie teeth, and a sack of potent herbs from around the world.

The commotion of battle intensified, but Umaq ignored the racket. Sweat soaked him as he shouted enchantments, waved his arms in spell casting, and drummed up spiritual energy through ritual dancing. The window flickered. The normal outside view swapped back and forth with images of darkness and fire. He sensed the barrier between the worlds tremble, yet it refused to break.

Umaq strained in renewed effort. He raised the medallion, and a bolt of lightning tore from the gem to blast through the window. No result. He sprinkled the dried puma blood in a circle and burned the specialized herbs inside it. Nothing happened. His throat grew dry and painful from endless mantras. Fatigue sagged his body and he trembled from exertion. He collapsed on the stone floor having nothing left. No more spells, ideas, or magical items remained.

"Umaq, Inti has the upper hand!" a frantic male voice called from the temple doorway. "He's broken through the demon line. The Maiden and Mama Quilla have joined the battle with Cessani, but the coven can't hold out much longer. Do something!"

Rage exploded inside Umaq. A pulse pounded in his temples. His hands curled into shaking fists. Do something? Did this red-robed witch from Cessani's coven not see the exhaustion on Umaq's sweaty face? Did the scattered spell ingredients and discarded talismans all over the floor not signify heavy spell crafting? What about the overpowering, acrid smell of burning herbs used in ritual? And never mind the flickering portal in the window.

"I will do something," Umaq said evenly. "But I'll need your help. Come."

Umaq moved to the wooden coffer. Concealing his actions, he reached inside and removed a dagger from its sheath. He spun and plunged the weapon into the man's chest.

"Is this enough effort?" Umaq snarled.

The coven member cried out and dropped to his knees. Eyes wide in shock, his bloody hands grasped the hilt as he toppled over in death.

Umaq wasted no time. Dragging the body to the window, he grunted and struggled to hoist the man onto the stone sill. With a final kick, he pushed the body through Uku-Pacha and fell backwards from a sudden gust of wind. He gagged from the horrid smell pouring through the window. The view of outside no longer flickered. Instead, the black mouth of an activated portal appeared! Flames danced along the edges of the square opening. Screams, growls, and guttural speaking sounded within.

"Nothing like a fresh sacrifice to get the job done," Umaq said in triumph. He walked out of the temple to find Cessani as the battle raged in the Central Plaza.

More than half of the demons had been killed. Inti's powerful beams of scorching light blasted out from the sphere to annihilate the monsters. On either side of the wide field, wood and stone rubble lay everywhere as the bordering buildings suffered heavy damage. Fires burned on the grass and in newly built structures with smoke curling into the sky. A few of Cessani's witches lay dead in unrecognizable piles of ash, an unfortunate but useful occurrence. Those deaths in the chaos of battle would provide cover for Umaq's murder of the coven member.

Wearing street clothes and black hair collected in a thick braid, Mama Quilla charged forward and slashed at Inti using a massive white sword illuminated by a lunar glow. A huge gash opened in the ball of light. Resembling a solar flare, a roar of fire lashed out at the moon goddess. She waved her arm, and a shiny white shield materialized to absorb the flames.

"Silly mate!" Inti's voice called out. "You will cease to exist with the others."

"Mate?" Mama Quilla asked. "How romantic. Animals have mates. I guess that's all I ever was to you. I didn't even qualify as your wife."

Quilla dashed forward and launched a furious exchange of sword swipes and shield blocks. Crackling flames burst outwards from Inti. Some she blocked and others charred her arms and legs. Long cuts opened on the sun god. Neither deity budged. The blows grew even more frenzied, but Umaq noticed the moon goddess received the worst of it. She wouldn't last long at this rate.

Somewhere in the ruckus, Cessani shouted a command. Umaq looked around and spotted the witch alongside her coven. Together, the group launched a barrage of spears crafted from water. Most of them dissipated in a hiss of steam just before reaching Inti. Others plowed into the sun god with little effect.

"Do it now, Persephone!" Mama Quilla shouted between blows.

A column of light appeared and vanished. In its place, the Maiden stood wearing the same outfit and style as Quilla to include her braided white hair. Umaq watched in wonder as a ring of milky stones floated around the Maiden's waist. The young goddess twirled like a ballerina and sent the stones hurtling toward the sun god.

The glowing shards pounded Inti, and he roared in the first sign of pain. Black cracks zigzagged across the giant ball. The coven molded their watery spears into one giant column the size of a telephone pole. Dripping, it rocketed forward and slammed halfway into one of the cracks. Mama Quilla leapt into the air and plowed her long sword into another dark fissure caused by the Maiden's attack.

"Nice coordination," Umaq said to himself. "But it won't be enough." He glanced back toward the temple and sensed a growing dark energy, the approach of his long-awaited vengeance. Any moment now.

The sphere of light exploded in a bright flash and roar of fire. Umaq winced and covered his eyes, then a fierce heat and wind knocked him to the ground. He climbed to his feet and saw the real Inti standing in the smoldering grass.

With the sphere destroyed, the sun god now presented in his humanoid form. A shiny headdress adorned by many gold-plated feathers from the rare *coraquenque* bird covered his head. Gold plates and leather had been fashioned into spaulders. Gold bands encircled his upper arms and wrists. A long, single piece of vicuna wool draped his body and a wide, jewel-speckled belt cinched the outfit at the waist. Heavy earrings tugged his earlobes. Leather and fur sandals wrapped his feet.

Dark eyes pierced in a severe expression as the sun god slowly inspected the area. He examined the new construction—much of it in ruins again—then settled his gaze on those before him. He transferred the enormous axe gripped in one hand to the other. It seemed momentary panic rooted everyone to the spot. No one spoke or reacted…until the Maiden shattered the silence.

"Ok, I'm outta here!" she called. "I think all we did was piss him off." The young moon goddess vanished in a flash of light.

"Persephone!" Cessani shouted, but the deity had left.

Mama Quilla shook her head as she adjusted the large sword and shield in her grip. "Reckless and unpredictable." The goddess then nodded at Inti. "And you're just as ugly as I remember."

"And you're just as foolish," he replied.

He sprang forward and swung the axe in a wide arc. The weapon crashed against Quilla's shield and sent a piece of it flying. The moon goddess retaliated with a sword thrust. Inti deflected the blow using an armored wrist. Switching to a double-handed grip on the axe, he spun and used momentum to try and chop Quilla in half. In a quick pivot, she kicked the wooden handle just below the blade and stopped the weapon.

"Umaq!" Cessani called, running toward him. The old witch looked tired, sweat moistening her face. Her robe hung shredded down one side, and a severe burn marred her left hand. "Why do you look so calm? What happened in the temple?"

"Be patient," he told her. "The portal is open, and they will come."

"So what are they waiting for?" she asked in alarm. "We're getting slaughtered out here!"

"They will swarm through the portal when gathered as a group," he answered. "The demon realm is vast. It's not like—"

Behind them, the front wall of the Temple of the Three Windows suddenly burst in a shower of granite blocks and wood. Stone flew in high arcs and wood shards spun off in all directions. Dust clouds rolled across the narrow paths between structures. Giant roars sounded amid the turmoil as a dark mass of creatures charged forth.

Umaq smiled. The growling mob raced past him and Cessani, a blast of wind and flying grit in their wake. These larger, stronger, and faster creatures represented an advanced hierarchy in the netherworld over the lesser demons he had summoned centuries ago. They moved with intellect and purpose, presented guile and strategy as opposed to mindless attack. Some creatures pounded the turf using cloven hooves. Others slapped the stone path with hairy feet or paws. At least three monsters slithered like snakes. Horns, claws, and jagged teeth adorned the mob. Whether smooth-skinned, half-rotted, or covered in scales, all demons appeared hideous and straight out of nightmares.

A cold hand clamped on Umaq's shoulder, and he turned. Golden eyes resembling a cat's stared into his. Mist rose from the smooth, charcoal-colored skin of a nude feminine form. No hair grew from her head. Instead of a nose, two small slits opened above her mouth. Four arms extended from her torso, and her feet resembled a bird's. Six breasts lined her chest in two rows of three. Bony spikes rose on each of her narrow shoulders. A horrid smell wafted from her body, the odor of putrid milk and festering meat.

"Uuumaaaq," the creature murmured. "Humans are so beneath me. Yet here I am under your control, humiliated to the point of pain. After I am free of your grasp, I will boil you for eternity."

"Shut up," he retorted, unimpressed. "That's not the first time a demon has said something like that to me. Now go and do your job, Zelaenah."

The female monster hissed. Two of her hands reached around Umaq's neck and stopped an inch from his skin, trembling in an effort to squeeze yet unable to. She finally screamed in rage and ran off to join the others.

"Goddess," Cessani breathed. Her face had grown pale, and she appeared ready to faint. "I thought I had gotten used to being around demons. But this new batch…" She trailed off and shook her head.

Mama Quilla and Inti hadn't ceased their heated battle. Sword and axe flailed in a steel dance. The broken shield moved up and down, forward and back in defense and attack. Quilla looked exhausted, black bangs plastered to her wet face. Wounds bled on her upper arms and thighs while Inti appeared unharmed.

Cessani's coven moved around the deities, glancing at each other in uncertainty. The witches scattered once the charging demons came into view. Risking a sideways glimpse, Mama Quilla shouted in surprise and rolled out of the way as the snarling creatures rushed the sun god.

Inti flailed his axe as demons slashed, bit, and struck his body. Amid the snarls and howls, the monsters moved in well-timed and coordinated attacks. The beasts even displayed feints from the ground while assailing the sun god from above. Some creatures fell dead at Inti's feet, heads and limbs severed. But the sustained brawl provided enough time for Umaq to prepare the final blow.

"Take a break if you want, Cessani," he said to the old witch. "It's my turn."

Umaq turned away from the melee and ran across the Sacred Plaza. Moving between the walls constructed of polygonal shaped rocks, he reached a series of winding steps surrounded by grassy, shelf-like terraces originally used for cultivation. Out of breath, he entered a small courtyard at the top of the hill and finally reached the ancient, ritual stone monument of Intihuatana.

"Where the sun is tied," he panted, expressing the stone block's meaning.

The monument featured a large, rectangular base with carved shelves, benches, and an elevated flat surface used as an altar. Powerful ley lines crossed Machu Picchu, and Intihuatana represented one of the focal points for the enormous mystical energy buried inside the earth. The altar served several purposes.

Having intricate surfaces and angles cut into the stone, subjects such as astronomy, a calendar to track seasonal events, and worshiping the sun god represented some of the monument's uses.

And now, Intihuatana would serve as the deity's grave.

Umaq hovered his palms just above the altar's surface. Closing his eyes, his mind burrowed deep into the earth and slipped into the spiritual energy pulsing beneath his feet. Digging farther, his awareness tore past the bedrock and crust of the land, thrust away soil and entrenched stone. Riding the wave of mystical power, he traveled *through* the planet and into an unimaginable void between worlds. His consciousness rushed past the earthly plane, cracked the flow of time, and tapped into the cold, black energy of the netherworld where demons dwelled. Soaking in the dark power source, he reversed course and drove the twisted essence back toward the stone monument.

Umaq drew a deep breath and shouted an incantation. *"Gods I defy and customs I break. Seas boil and mountains quake. My power within and throughout the unknown, I shall bind the sun god to the dark stone!"*

Intihuatana started to glow in a murky hue. Raw, black energy from the nether rose like smoke as Umaq continued the spell. *"Hear my call to the darkness below. By blood, by defiance, my mind and with might. Cast down my nemesis, for the sun god I blight!"*

A thick, twisting beam of darkness blasted forth from the altar. The black column soared through the air in a wide arc and crashed onto Inti in the midst of his battle. Like a long tether, the cold energy connected the sun god to the monument. From the hill, Umaq looked down into the Central Plaza as Inti struggled against the beam's pull.

Demons continued their relentless assault, their presence invaluable as the sun god weakened. Being yanked toward the altar by the spell, the deity's feet dragged across the turf while he deflected blows and tried to break free.

"This is ludicrous!" Inti shouted as he dropped to a knee. "I am the sun. The very star fire that blinds and incinerates all!"

A powerful light erupted around the god. Umaq threw an arm over his eyes and grunted from intense heat. The brightness diminished and he glanced down into the valley, his skin stinging as if he had passed through fire. A few more demons and witches lay dead, but the spell had not failed. The black leash still held Inti and tugged him further.

"The sun burns in my wrath!" the deity hollered.

Flames coated his body, and he used spurts of fire to try and sever the dark cord. After several futile attempts, he flew high into the air and strained against the incantation as the tether stretched into a thin line.

The spell weakened as the fire intensified the harder the god resisted. Umaq slammed his hands onto the altar and tried to siphon more dark magic. The excruciating effort strained the limits of his mind and body. His head seemed to split in pain. An invisible weight crushed his shoulders. The bones in his arms and legs neared the breaking point as he struggled to stand. Nausea threatened to make him vomit. Darkness clouded his vision. Battling a swoon, he suddenly felt a relief in pressure when a commotion sounded in the sky.

Exhausted, Umaq leaned on the altar and gazed up at Inti. A second figure had appeared in the air above him—the Maiden with something resembling a large garbage can in her arms. The moon goddess flipped upside down and dumped a giant cloud of gray powder all over the sun god.

"Time for a lunar dust bath!" she shouted, her white braid dangling down and sneakers toward the sky.

A loud hiss emanated around Inti as the powder doused the roaring flames on his body. The black tether strengthened and resumed its pull. Inti thrashed in its grasp and shouted in fury.

Another person soared into the picture. Mama Quilla renewed her salvo of sword thrusts and shield slams. Caught in Intihuatana's dark grasp, the sun deity barely managed to defend himself with his axe. Quilla moved and struck carefully, trying to keep Inti busy as he drew closer to the stone monument.

Umaq's elation intensified. The dark magic continued to drag the sun god closer until he hovered fifty yards above. Once Inti reached the altar, the final blow would strike to send the deity into oblivion.

Umaq reached into the black mass swirling out of the stone. He grasped a handful of the darkness and fashioned the essence into a razor-sharp dagger. The mystical weapon possessed the ability to end the sun god, but only after he lay on top of the altar. Looking upwards, Umaq paced the length of the monument in restless anticipation.

With Zelaenah in the lead, the demon horde ascended the final flight of stairs and bounded into the courtyard. The creatures howled, barked, and growled up at the captured deity as he struggled against the tether and Mama Quilla's attacks. Zelaenah folded all four of her arms and calmly watched the show. Behind the monsters, Cessani and her coven joined the crowd around the stone monument. Persephone floated down and studied her nails.

"I can't believe it's over with," said Cessani. "You've done it, Umaq."

"Impossible without your help," he admitted. "Even the moon goddesses came through."

He glanced back up to the fray and gasped. Inti suddenly penetrated Quilla's defense and smashed her with the axe. Umaq dodged shards of broken shield and Mama Quilla herself as the moon deity crashed onto the altar and rolled off onto the ground, unmoving.

Tiny flames danced in Inti's eyes as he shot everyone a hate-filled gaze. "I will end this now!" the deity roared only twenty feet above the altar. He reached back to throw the axe toward Umaq, but an explosion from the roof of a nearby temple halted him.

A bright blue light blasted from the opening in the roof and rocketed into the sky. The hilltop shook in a violent quake. Pieces of the roof rained down in the courtyard. The startled demons ran about in chaos. Umaq and the witches regained their footing, then stared at the massive fountain of light.

"It's a ruptured ley line!" Cessani exclaimed. "This shouldn't be happening, it's not natural. If the unrestricted energy intensifies, half of Machu Picchu will explode. We need to get out of here!"

"No, we're too close to victory," Umaq urged.

He sensed something else spurting from the broken ley line, a strange energy not part of the earth's spirit. The foreign sensation grew, which meant the source of the unnatural energy quickly approached. "There's something coming through!"

He checked the altar and found Inti standing on the surface. The black leash held him tight, but the deity managed to raise the axe and chop the stone in an attempt to destroy the monument. A few chunks of Intihuatana sailed in all directions. One piece struck Umaq on the forehead and knocked him unconscious.

Chapter Nine

Scorched Plans, Revisited

Sybil screamed. Her body burned as if on fire, then trembled from severe cold. She spun in terrible darkness or floated in light too intense to observe. Ear-splitting rumbles of earth threatened to crack her skull. Long, terrifying silences overwhelmed her with dread and loneliness. Having lost control of the ley line, Sybil and her friends tumbled helplessly along the mystical river of the planet's essence.

A hot wind fluttered her hair as the vivid scene changed all around. She flew high over ancient Egypt as thousands of workers moved great limestone blocks. An incomplete pyramid dominated the landscape. Blue ley line energy spewed from the unfinished top. In an unexpected panic, she shouted down to the workers and urged them to stop the planet from bleeding.

The environment changed again. Sybil now flew through a rainstorm high over ancient England. As in Egypt, thousands of workers hauled many massive sandstones and bluestones across the landscape to build Stonehenge. Lightning flashed and thunder boomed. Trapped within the unfinished circle of stones, blue ley line essence roared and spun in a violent tornado of energy. Desperate to quell the Earth's wound, she tried to yell a warning at the workers over the roar of the storm.

The scenery transformed, and Sybil sailed over the Nazca Lines etched into a desert in southern Peru. A giant hummingbird, spider, condor, monkey, and other zoomorphic designs painted the vast terrain. Other mysterious and beautiful glyphs adorned the ground in geometric shapes. An ancient people moved over the ground, manipulating the sand and earth to create more pictures. High in the air, an odd silver machine floated with blinking lights. A ruptured ley line stretched from the ground to the spherical machine as it absorbed the planet's energy. The floating object terrified Sybil as she realized the thing did not belong to this world.

"Sybil! Where are we, what's happening? Will this ever end?"

She heard a faint voice as Nazca and all her surroundings faded into a blue mist. She zoomed along in a void where nothing existed. Not even her, as she glanced down and didn't see her own body. Did her consciousness travel in some strange plane?

"Marcelo?" she called in desperation. "Johann? Salix?"

A wind blew and leaves rustled, but how could that be inside oblivion? Yet tremendous relief flooded her as Salix's voice entered her mind. *Fear not, Spell Weaver. The journey is almost finished. The Earth Mother has been wounded by our effort. Ley line essence spills like a ruptured vein. I feel Her distress. I am troubled.*

Disembodied, Sybil didn't require a heart to experience unbearable grief. The emotion crushed her beneath its unforgiving boot.

"Salix, I am so sorry!" she cried out into the nothing. "I did not intend to cause harm, I warrant. I shall make everything better, I promise!"

The surrounding blue mist shifted to form a tunnel ahead. A light glimmered inside—the way out. Sybil's physical form returned as she raced toward the opening, arms and legs waving. Marcelo, Johann, and Salix appeared close by and sailed along with her. Sybil didn't have a chance to speak before everyone blasted through the tunnel and out into the real world.

The group tumbled to the stone floor of a destroyed building. The roof had been blasted out as blue ley line energy roared into the sky beside them in a giant column. Through the jagged opening, intense sunlight poured into the room.

Marcelo yelled as his body smoked and erupted in flame. In a frenzy, he sped out through the ruined doorway and out of sight. Salix sprinted after him. Johann exchanged a look of horror with Sybil, then both ran outside into chaos.

Reaching a courtyard, Sybil stopped in shock. In a few seconds, she absorbed a vast amount of data that left her head spinning. On a large hilltop that she recognized from a photo of Machu Picchu, her group had stumbled upon a battle against the sun god, Inti. Umaq sat on the ground, a hand pressed to his bleeding forehead. Standing on a stone altar and bound by the waist through some sort of dark energy, the irate sun god thrashed and bellowed. Horrible demons slashed, bit, and bludgeoned Inti as he wildly swung an axe. Cessani and her coven cast chains made of ice and lunar light. They wove them around Inti's wrists and ankles to further subdue the deity. Off to the side, Sybil recognized the young goddess of the moon, the Maiden, carefully dragging another unconscious moon deity away from the brawl.

Marcelo's burning body fell down a nearby flight of stairs. He rolled over the stone steps and landed on one of the grassy terraces cut into the side of the tall hill. Salix leapt down after him and spread her arms. Huge, thick leaves grew from her arms, legs, and torso until she resembled a giant green bush. The dryad threw herself on top of Marcelo to smother the flames, then remained on him to block the sun.

On his knees, Umaq gestured weakly and a few of the demons left the altar to chase after Marcelo and Salix.

"Go and save the sun god," Johann said quickly. "I'll protect Marcelo and Salix."

He ran toward the demons and shifted into a bounding, snarling werewolf. He collided against the monsters and burst into a feverish exchange of fangs and claws.

Sybil's heart thundered in terror as she thought of Marcelo. How severe were his injuries? Night should have greeted them, not broad daylight. She longed to be at his side, but a glance at the altar didn't allow time to ponder her lover's condition or what had gone wrong during the ley line journey. Bound and helpless, Inti now lay on the stone block. Umaq stood over the deity, a black dagger raised.

Sybil snapped into action. She extended an arm toward the gushing ley line, and a portion of blue mist zoomed to her hand. The essence hardened in her palm, and with a grunt, she launched the shard toward Umaq. The chunk of ley line zig-zagged around combatants, between legs, over shoulders, and smashed into his raised arm. He shouted in pain as the black dagger spun from his grip and landed across the plaza.

"Cessani, Zelaenah, stop that bratty girl!" Umaq shouted. "I'll finish off Inti."

"Maintain your hold on those chains," Cessani commanded her coven.

She then motioned at Sybil, and a spiked ball of ice flew from the older witch's hand. Sybil dove to the ground and the barbed, frozen orb shattered against the ruined building behind her.

A foul odor wafted close, and she suddenly rolled to one side even though Cessani had not attacked again. A rush of wind passed overhead as something narrowly missed Sybil. She glanced up and spotted a female demon leaping onto a partially crumbled wall, its bird talons gripping the stone. Gold cat-eyes glared as mist rose from its obsidian-colored skin. The creature's horrid smell had given the monster away before the failed strike.

Sybil waved an arm to manipulate the broken ley fountain. A section of blue mist hardened into a thick staff. The makeshift weapon flipped end over end and clubbed the demon on the back of its head. The monster fell from its perch and crashed on the ground.

An opponent down, Sybil ran toward Cessani. The old witch launched a much larger spiked ball of ice. Without breaking her stride, Sybil reached back to absorb more ley energy from the ruptured fountain. The blue mist collected in her hand, and she formed the essence into a crude sword. The ley blade smashed through the ice ball in an explosion of frozen splinters.

Ignoring the cuts to her face and arms, she swung the sword at Cessani. The elder witch held her ground and summoned a solid white column humming in lunar power. The ley weapon sliced into the pillar and embedded halfway. Sybil released the hilt and swept around the post. She grabbed Cessani's hair and punched her in the nose. The witch cried out and collapsed on the floor.

Sybil panicked as she spotted Umaq sprinting to the altar, black dagger in hand after he'd found it amid the bedlam. He raised the weapon to stab the sun god. Spreading her arms wide, tiny bolts of lightning tickled her palms and danced across her fingers. The miniature lightning raced up her arms and down her body until crackling light enveloped her. Thunder boomed in the plaza as she teleported to his side in an instant.

She grabbed Umaq's wrist, and the pair wrestled for control. Clothes tore. Fingernails cut. Blows rained. Feet tangled as they danced in a heated struggle. He shoved her against the stone altar. She countered with a hard bite to his hand. The unexpected move worked as he hollered, and the blade clattered on the ground.

"Sybil, watch out!" Johann shouted.

She glanced back and saw Johann in human form. A demon's large cloven hoof pinned him to the ground. His body lay slashed, punctured, and bleeding. Icy dread formed in her gut as she recalled his werewolf form couldn't last long in the sun—another catastrophic mistake she made while using the ley line.

Two demons rushed Sybil before she had a chance to react to Johann's warning. Serrated teeth clamped around her forearm. A swiping claw ripped open her thigh. From behind, a terrible pain burst in her side as Umaq pushed the black dagger into her body.

Sybil fell onto the stone floor. All sound grew muffled, and tears blurred her vision. Johann's hazy body lay still, demons howling around him. Weak and disoriented, she dragged herself to the edge of the plaza to look for Marcelo. On the grassy terrace below, Salix had remained on top of Marcelo to protect him with her hardened leaf shield. A knot of demons hammered at the green barrier and tore pieces away. The dryad grew the vegetation back in an instant, but Sybil knew the frenzied onslaught of claws and teeth would soon break through.

No longer able to move, she squinted at the altar. Umaq faced the stone block and slammed his dark blade deep into Inti's chest. The sun god roared and struggled in his restraints. A moment later, a massive column of fire rocketed into the sky from the deity's body. Powerful heat and dancing flames radiated. Umaq, Cessani, and the other witches sprinted for cover.

The blazing pillar vanished. The charred altar stood empty with no sign of the sun god. Umaq and the others slowly emerged from hiding. He looked into the sky and shouted in triumph, both arms in the air. A smiling Cessani and her coven exchanged hugs.

"Marcelo," Sybil whispered in grief.

It was over. Only death could take her pain away. She had failed the mission, lost her friends to darkness, and murdered the love of her life in utter carelessness.

Next to her head, a pair of black bird talons stepped into view. One of the talons gripped Sybil's shoulder and flipped her onto her back. She stared up at the obsidian-skinned demon, the one Umaq called

Zelaenah. A putrid smell surrounded the naked, four-armed and six-breasted female.

"I will not miss this time," the demon said, raising a large rock over Sybil.

Many beams of dazzling light suddenly burst throughout the plaza. The rods of illumination plowed into the demons and sent them scattering in surprise. One ray struck Zelaenah's chest and knocked her over.

Sybil fought to remain conscious. She had lost a large amount of blood, and just taking a breath proved excruciating. The strange activity around her faded into the distance. Her world transformed into a fuzzy dream. She couldn't even determine if what she now witnessed was real.

Amid the falling beams of light, two women dressed in white gowns hurried across the plaza. One of them bent down to touch Johann's body; he then disappeared in a bright flash. The second woman leapt down to the grassy terrace where Marcelo and Salix lay. She enveloped them within a soft glow, and all three disappeared.

The woman who made Johann vanish stood over Sybil. Long white hair curtained the sides of her smooth face and drifted over her shoulders to mid-back. Cobalt eyes looked down in sympathy. She bent and scooped Sybil into her arms as illumination blazed all around.

Sybil managed a final word before the light faded to dark. "Mother…"

***

Something cold splashed over Sybil's bare feet, and she began to wake. She listened to the roar of water and the cry of a gull. The smell of salt lingered in the air. She recognized the loud clap of a wave hitting the shore, and a moment later, sea water splashed around her feet again. A clear blue sky met her eyes when she opened them. Sitting up, she winced as pain throbbed on her forearm, thigh, and right side—her injuries during the battle with Umaq.

Memory rushed back, and Sybil rose slowly. Someone had dressed her in a loose gown and tended her wounds. A soft white light of healing glowed from bandages wrapped over the places she had been hurt. The pain had grown tolerable; however, no treatment existed for the agony in her heart.

"Marcelo!" she cried, glancing around.

She stood in Avila Beach, or at least a replica of it where she lived with Marcelo. An odd feeling of hollowness existed here. The cold water and white sand, the blue sky with gulls, and the smell of salt seemed real enough, but instinct told her otherwise.

"Marcelo is resting," a disembodied voice said.

Sybil turned but didn't see anyone. "Resting?" Intense relief washed over her like the wave hitting her ankles. The powerful sensation nearly dropped her to her knees. A tear fell down her cheek, and she wiped it away. Her heart fluttered in anticipation as she dared ask her next question. "And my other friends…how do they fare?"

"I have not seen the Reaper, so I imagine your friends will recover as well," the voice answered.

A heavy burden of sorrow lifted from Sybil's shoulders. She leaned over, hands pressed to her knees and took several calming breaths. After regaining her composure, she rose and a woman in a white gown materialized on the sand. Back in Machu Picchu, a sense of recognition had hit Sybil just as she lost consciousness in this woman's arms. Having prayed to moon deities her entire life, the familiarity returned at once.

Sybil inclined her head in respect. "Mother of the Triple Moon Goddess. Truly, I have no words to express my gratitude. I—"

"Save it," the Mother responded, her expression and tone stern.

She stepped closer to the ocean as a wave crashed on the sand. The water rushed in and retreated in a foamy roar. "The Crone and I are not heroines. We are not warriors. Inti the sun god is dead, and Umaq has won. I only got involved because I took pity on Grace, so there is nothing to be thankful for."

"Grace?" Sybil asked in surprise. "Is she well? Wherefore does this have to do with her?"

A breeze wavered the Mother's long white hair and fluttered the hem of her gown. "Despite Grace facing adversity in and around Salem, that strong-spirited witch still had the gall to approach the Crone and I while asking us to intervene in Umaq's affairs. I told Grace the moon goddesses don't choose sides. But after the Maiden turned rogue, I suppose something had to be done. Besides, there's an archetype to uphold, as your friend pointed out. We *are* the Triple Moon Goddess…not the Double and the Single. The Maiden must return and the unity sustained."

Grace, what an amazing and courageous witch! She had somehow convinced the lunar deities to act, even if their purpose represented selfish reasons. But worry gripped Sybil over the distressing news about her friend experiencing trouble. Cessani's coven must still be causing problems in Salem. Sybil yearned to see Grace. After what happened at Machu Picchu, she swore never to place a friend in danger like that again.

"Mother, my heart is still very grateful to you and the Crone," said Sybil. "I need not be conversant with your reasons, but of a truth, you saved our lives." When the Mother didn't respond, Sybil continued. "Where do we dwell, exactly? How long have we stayed hither?"

"As a gifted witch, you may have surmised we are not truly in Avila Beach," the Mother replied. "We are in a realm where deities wander, though your surroundings reflect what you deeply desire. You long to be home with the one you love. For five days you have slept on this beach. You looked so peaceful during recovery, I left you here on the sand."

Five days in the celestial realm. After the fall of a sun god, Sybil could only imagine what had been happening in the world during that time. "Please, I wish to have a fair sight of my friends."

The goddess turned away from the water and looked toward the residential area beyond the strip of beach. "You know where to go."

Sybil hurried across the sand and continued on San Rafael Street. Only a short distance from the ocean, she reached Marcelo's beautiful home in the quiet and secluded neighborhood. She headed through an iron gateway and jogged up the long, curved driveway. Inside the spacious foyer, a motion sensor activated a crystal chandelier as she stepped across white marble tile swirled with blue.

She opened the double doors to the master bedroom and halted. Marcelo lay on the bed, his half-nude body charred black in several places. The goddess of the waning moon, the Crone, stood next him and waved a hand over a miniature moon that hovered above the bed. Light from the white sphere bathed Marcelo in a gentle radiance. The illumination matched the glow from Sybil's bandages, and she understood the Crone had worked hard to heal her and Marcelo.

"The dead man lives, as ironic as that sounds," said the Crone. "His body may look like a mess, but he's improved quite a bit. He has yet to wake up, however. Just a little more time."

"I am in your debt, Goddess," Sybil replied as she moved to Marcelo's side.

"I'll give you two some space," the Crone said as she left the room.

Sybil grasped Marcelo's cold hand. The sun had been cruel as it burned and blistered his body. He looked so fragile on the bed, and his face did not appear at rest. Was he in pain? Did horrible dreams haunt his sleep?

Powerful guilt and heavy grief buckled Sybil's legs. She knelt on the floor and cried into Marcelo's pale, limp hand. She had nearly killed him! Her overconfidence had done this. How could she have been so careless with the ley line? Time had somehow warped during the experimental journey. Instead of the ride lasting a few moments after leaving Oregon, several hours had been lost and placed their arrival well into the following day.

Inti the sun god is dead, and Umaq has won. The Mother's haunting words echoed in Sybil's mind. Her failure had led to evil's triumph. What would happen to the world now? Where to go from here? Those questions could be set aside. For the moment, Sybil only cared about Marcelo's recovery and the wellbeing of her friends.

Wiping her eyes, she gazed around the master bedroom and studied the beautiful wood furniture, pictures, and decorations. Their real home had been partially destroyed during the fight against the demon assassin, but this restored copy in the celestial plane matched every detail and placement. Certificates and plaques hung on the walls, each one a gift from various cities describing Marcelo's noble contributions to their community. Over the years, he had donated to schools, libraries, hospitals, police, and fire departments, to name a few. The inscriptions spoke of the enhanced lives of citizens, but for Sybil, his absolute love represented her true reward. Kissing the back of his hand, she left the room and found the Mother and Crone speaking in the living room.

"Your other friends are in the backyard," the Mother announced before Sybil could ask. "The dryad cannot remain here much longer, but I'll let her explain why. As for Johann, his physical injuries will heal. But with Inti's death and nature's balance destroyed, the power of the moon has been amplified. As a werewolf having a synergistic connection to the moon, the spike in power will affect his mental state."

"Like he's intoxicated," the Crone added. "It might be difficult for him to transform or even think clearly. And that's for both human and werewolf states. The Mother and I have tried to find a cure, but nature's imbalance—as well as the Maiden's departure—have seriously hampered our ability to function."

Another wave of guilt tore through Sybil and turned her stomach. Johann's condition marked another result of her failure to stop Umaq. She should be the one injured in bed or feeling moon-drunk, not her dear friends.

"Truly, I appreciate the helpful information and kindness, Goddesses," she said before heading outside.

In the spacious patio lined by palm trees and bushes, Sybil found Salix standing in the grass beneath the sunlight. Patches of bark and leaves had been torn from the dryad's small body. Ugly wounds dominated her green olive skin. Several branches on her head had been broken off. Exhaustion and sorrow dwelled in her distant gaze. However, Salix's vivid emerald eyes exhibited joy and relief when Sybil approached.

Sybil held the dryad in a tight hug. She inhaled the aroma of fresh grass, rich moist soil, and honey mixed with lemon. She kissed Salix where her mouth would have been and pressed her forehead against her friend's. "My heart breaks for you, dear dryad. I can never ask for forgiveness."

Salix brushed a moss-covered finger across Sybil's cheek, the soft rasp her words. *Forgiveness is not necessary, Spell Weaver. You have committed no transgression. All wounds over Earth, body, and spirit will heal. I am patient.*

Sybil pulled back and wiped a teary eye. "Then I shall be as well, my friend. But the Mother hath mentioned you are going forth? Truly, I do not wish to see you depart."

To communicate, Salix scraped a fingernail across a hard patch of bark on her forearm. *The moon goddesses have been helpful. But to recover properly, I must rest in my home surrounded by Salix delnortensis.*

The Mother will transport me. The healing is not long and I will see you again, Spell Weaver. I am certain.

Sybil hugged the dryad again. "I shall always think of you and look forth to our next meeting."

Salix nodded, then pointed across the large yard. In the farthest corner, Sybil spotted Johann in werewolf form lying in the shade of a tree. A small moon similar to the one in Marcelo's room floated over him, its healing light covering the werewolf in a wide beam.

She turned to the dryad to ask about Johann's condition, but Salix had gone inside, more than likely ready to depart. Sybil walked to Johann and he opened his eyes; an absent gaze seemed to look through her at nothing. A deep growl rumbled in the werewolf's chest. Goosebumps rose on Sybil's skin, and she took a step back.

Recognition appeared within Johann's eyes. He shuddered in the grass and whined as if in pain. Transforming, the blond fur on his body receded to reveal soft flesh. The canine features smoothed into the familiar human shape of his face and limbs. Breathing heavily, he lay naked in a fetal position, his body marked by injuries from the demon attacks. The wounds appeared to be fading in a positive sign the moonlight treatment had worked.

Sybil knelt in the grass and placed a comforting hand on his shoulder. "I fear you are still in discomfort. I shall find the Crone."

Johann grabbed her wrist before she could stand. "No. I'm fine, Sybil." He struggled into a sitting position, the blond hair loose around his face and shoulders. "I'm sorry if I startled you. The mystical imbalance has made my head fuzzy. I feel out of place, and lost. Transforming takes a ton of effort. Or like yesterday, it happened without me wanting it to."

"Johann, I…" Sybil fought back another round of tears. A deep sigh of remorse lifted her shoulders. "Of a truth, my error with yonder ley line…'twas inexcusable. All of you could have—"

"Hey, say no more, sweet thing," Johann said. "Look. No other method would have gotten us all the way to the southern hemisphere and past Umaq's defenses. You presented the team with a viable option, and we all knew the risks. And do you know the best part?" He paused, smiling. "We may not have arrived the night before, but we still got there in time. We had a chance, Sybil, and that's all that matters. I saw you trading blows with Umaq and felt very proud. I know Marcelo is, too. When he gets his lazy butt up, he will tell you himself."

Sybil's dear friends had been so kind and understanding, but she didn't deserve their support. It might have been easier if at least one of them screamed at her in anger. Nevertheless, a mountain of stress tumbled free from her heart. Rough spots in her consciousness produced by sorrow had been smoothed over by relief. With emotions spinning and words eluding her, she threw her arms around Johann and kissed his cheek.

He gently patted her on the back. "Thank you for visiting this nude patient in the psycho ward."

Heat rushed into Sybil's cheeks, and she pulled back in sudden awareness. "I…well…"

Johann laughed. "I'm sorry. I think the Crone hid my clothes on purpose. She might be into me."

Sybil laughed for the first time in what seemed ages. "Thank you, Johann." She looked around the well-manicured patio. "Salix hath gone forth, and I must depart for Salem to aid a friend in danger. Shall you remain hither to recover?"

Johann leapt to his feet, and Sybil's cheeks flushed again. He strode to a lawn chair and picked up a pile of folded garments. "I knew where my clothes were all this time, but so what? The Crone having the hots for me seemed a more interesting story."

He began to dress. "I'm going with you, Sybil. No way am I lounging around here with the world a mess. My injuries feel better. Plus, you mentioned danger, and Marcelo would skin me if I let you do this alone." He finished lacing his shoes. "I'm ready when you are."

Johann abruptly cried out in severe pain. Eyes squeezed shut, a hand flew to his temple and he sat down hard on the lawn chair. Alarmed, Sybil raced to his side and placed an arm around his shoulders. He blinked several times and forced a smile. "Just a little headrush, nothing to worry about."

"Johann, perhaps you ought to remain hither," Sybil suggested. "Yonder moon's unbalanced energy hath affected you. The Goddesses—"

"I know, I know," he replied. "The deities have said enough. I'm intoxicated. Overdosed. Poisoned. But I need to get out of here, Sybil. Laying around is making it worse. Some fresh air and activity in Salem will do wonders, you'll see. Let's go help your friend while Marcelo and Salix recover."

Sybil hesitated. She didn't want to jeopardize Johann's recovery when he really should be resting.

However, the longing in his gaze and urgency in his voice persuaded her to agree. She would keep a close eye on him, but perhaps some time away and a distraction would in fact help. And if Cessani's witches have been causing trouble in Salem, a werewolf at Sybil's side would be most welcome.

She smiled and patted his shoulder. "Then let us go forth. I shall make you conversant about Grace when we arrive." She glanced down at the gown the deities had dressed her in. "I shall change clothing and meet you in yonder living room."

In the master bedroom, Sybil gazed at Marcelo's prone body as she unbuttoned the gown. It slipped off her shoulders and fell around her ankles. She moved to the bed and carefully laid down next to him. Her fingers caressed his face, slid down his chest, and a palm rubbed over his midsection. She placed her leg between his, her heart and breath quickening as she cuddled him.

Sybil gently kissed his mouth, and whispered in his ear. "I love you, Marcelo. We shall be together soon."

Rising from the bed, she unwrapped the glowing bandages on her forearm, thigh, and side to inspect the healing wounds. The level of pain still felt bearable as it did upon waking on the beach. She dressed, and silently thanked the moon goddesses when she found her phone and Salix's twig on the nightstand. Prepared, Sybil left the room and found the Mother in the foyer.

"You need me to transfer you and the werewolf to Salem," the goddess stated. "I will comply, but this is the final time the Crone and I will become involved in your affairs. You're on your own from now on."

Sybil nodded, not really surprised based on her conversation with the deity on the beach. "I understand,

Mother, and appreciate all you have done hither. I only hope you and the Crone shall soon be reunited with the Maiden."

Johann approached, and the Mother studied them both for a moment. With nothing more to say, the goddess waved her arm, and a shining portal to Salem appeared in the doorway.

Chapter Ten

Blue Gates & Black Portals

Umaq stood on the charred and broken altar at Intihuatana. Several days ago, Inti lay bound beneath his feet and the sun god's light had been extinguished. After defeating his centuries-old rival, Umaq felt damn good. It amused him that in all the movies and TV shows, someone always begged the hero not to kill their adversary. *Revenge won't bring little Billy back*, or *Murder is not the answer; don't stoop to the bad guy's level.* He laughed. Revenge was the *only* answer. Exhilaration and relief flooded his veins. It felt as if he could leap off the stone monument and fly in elation.

From the hilltop where the final battle had taken place, Machu Picchu stretched out before him on this clear day. Construction resumed as the remaining lesser demons toiled to rebuild the damage from the clash with Inti. Stacking stone and cutting wood proved easy, yet no entity could repair the harm triggered by the death of a sun god.

The power of the sun had waned, but only on a mystical level. For the majority of normal humans, they wouldn't detect any real physical changes to their environment. To them, the sun continued to shine and brighten the sky as always. However, the true darkness brought by Inti's demise lay in the barriers between worlds. Spiritual borders thinned and walls cracked. Supernatural beings across all planes stirred, but those lurking in the blackness of the netherworld were Umaq's target for liberation.

Below in the Sacred Plaza, a light flashed from within the restored Temple of the Three Windows. A moment later, two scaly, horned demons scampered through the doorway. They paused to sniff the air, glanced about, then charged off to join their comrades in the grassy Central Plaza.

The random flashing light had been the portal reactivating for a short time, a surprising and welcomed side effect of Umaq's efforts. He realized the gateway had not disappeared after its initial use when Zelaenah and the others had come through. Instead, the window portal occasionally activated on its own. It blinked into existence for a few seconds or up to several minutes at a time.

Some ferocious demons had taken advantage of the sporadic openings to push through. The creatures immediately fell under Umaq's command, and through that connection, he sensed the monsters' desire to infest this world and conquer it—a perfect attitude that matched his wish to continue the assault.

Not completely satisfied with Inti's fall, Machu Picchu represented only a sliver of what Umaq could have. Sitting back now and sipping drinks did not suit him. He envisioned demonic armies at his side and the world at his feet. His ancient quarrel against Inti provided an example of why he despised the old gods— useless, obsolete, and insignificant in the modern world.

The time had arrived for a new god, a flesh and blood representative of the mortal plane.

The broken portal offered a path to success, but the periodic openings posed a problem. Umaq needed a permanent gateway, a wide-open mouth to vomit demonic entities and spill malevolence into the streets. Enchantments, rituals, potions, and even more human sacrifices simply would not work. Shattering the barrier between worlds required more darkness, and only one method sufficed.

The fall of another sun god.

Blighting the illumination of an additional solar deity would flood the world in mystical night and maintain the portal open. Umaq could then reach deep into the netherworld and scrape its bowels for the most powerful beasts and dark demigods. With the world as his playground, everyone would comprehend the true destiny of Umaq the Betrayer.

The sound of a helicopter disturbed his musing. At a presumed safe distance, a single news chopper dared hover near the citadel to film the activity. Umaq allowed it. He hoped their cameras had a good zoom function. He needed the exposure to inform the world of who held the true power. The news outlets must have caught amazing footage of the battle against Inti. The military forces had even pulled back. Not a single camouflaged vehicle, soldier, or mortar had come near Machu Picchu in nearly a week.

The helicopter left. Umaq stepped off the altar and headed toward the ruined building where Sybil and her group had emerged. The one-room structure had been a temple during his time with the Inca, but remained unused since the rebuilding of Machu Picchu. Now it lay in ruins again courtesy of the ruptured ley line. The fountain of earth energy had finally subsided, and the ground sealed itself. Umaq still couldn't believe Sybil had appeared in such dramatic fashion. Clearly the witch had miscalculated and lost control, but it still irritated him that she had somehow opened a ley gate and managed to travel here. Only he should have that knowledge and no one else.

He had spent several hours a day on the hilltop trying to solve how to reopen the ley gate. The earth energy had left behind residue in the form of solid blue pieces or glowing puddles of blue essence. He had collected the liquid into a few buckets and piled the shards into a large mass on the stone floor of the building. He discovered the shards were very fragile; they could be ground into powder, filed into shapes, or melted. The liquid could also be frozen and boiled. However, endless experimentation had not revealed how to open the ley line and his frustration mounted.

Umaq picked up a shard and stood next to the sealed fissure in the center of the temple. He waved a hand over the blue glassy stone, chanted, and drew patterns in the air. A curse flew from his mouth as the chunk of ley line suddenly burned his hand. He threw the blue piece at a partially crumbled wall, and it exploded in fragments.

Laughter sounded behind him. "Nice try," the demon Zelaenah said. "You'll never learn how to open a ley gate. It's quite different than opening portals."

"Don't you have better things to do than spy on me?" Umaq asked in a near shout. "You know I don't like to be disturbed while I work. Go supervise the reconstruction and double check those defenses. The military may have retreated, but now is not the time to let our guard down. After the battle with Inti, we don't want mortals outside the walls believing we've grown complacent."

Zelaenah hissed and bared her sharp teeth at the command. After spreading her four arms, the lower two molded into her torso. She bent over and grunted as two feathery black wings burst from her narrow back—replacements for the consumed arms.

The shape-shifting demon beat her wide wings toward Umaq. The wind ruffled his clothing and carried her foul odor. He recoiled from the stench and spat on the ground.

"And take a bath!" he yelled as she took flight, screeching.

Umaq shook his throbbing hand and used the other to sift through the pile of blue stones. He spotted a long, thicker piece he had dumped here earlier and pulled it out. About the length of his arm, he lazily swung it around while trying to think of another way to open the ley line. He stopped pacing after several frustrating moments and scooped up a smaller shard. To blow off some steam, he tossed the small piece in the air and swung the long rod to try and hit a homerun over the opposite crumbled wall.

The blue pole struck the smaller chunk and launched it out of the temple through the fallen roof. The rod in his hands vibrated from the impact and emitted a high-pitched sound like a fork striking a crystal glass. Umaq gasped as a crack appeared in the stone floor. Blue ley energy shone from within. A second later, the gap sealed.

Inspiration surged, and he struck the end of the rod onto the ground. The ley pole vibrated, but the high pitch from before failed to sound. He grabbed another shard and used the rod to hit the piece over the wall. The high-pitched tone sang in the ruined temple. The small fissure opened in the floor. Blue light flashed into view, then disappeared.

Umaq's heart raced in excitement. He collected a third fragment, but instead of hitting it over the wall, he simply struck the smaller piece against the longer rod to make it vibrate. The high-pitched tone rang. The ground opened and slammed shut after only a second.

"Frequency," he said to the empty ruins. "But how to sustain the right tone?"

Umaq hurried to his chambers and sketched several versions of a staff. He detailed the length, thickness, and some models even had dual prongs similar to a tuning fork. He instructed worker demons to craft several stone molds based on the drawings, and to build a small forge inside the ruined temple atop the hill.

***

Hours into the night, Umaq toiled at the forge. Sparks flew. Heat soaked him in sweat. The blue shards melted, and liquid poured into the molds to harden. Afterwards, he chipped and sanded any anomalies in the staffs to ensure smooth, unimpeded vibrations. The painstaking effort required steady hands and a delicate touch, something a mindless, clumsy demon lacked. His frantic work continued with no knowledge of time or when he had last eaten.

Several frequency tests arrived next. He selected various staff lengths and struck the ends using an apple-sized piece of blue ley stone. Different tones sounded. Sometimes nothing happened, but during other trials, the ley gate opened for several seconds longer than the first occasion. The size of the gate changed as well, depending on the staff's build.

Failed rods returned to the forge fire, and Umaq labored several hours more. Repeated molds were cut differently the next round, the shafts filed down or thinned at certain points. More tests. New tones rang in the destroyed temple. Cracks opened in the floor, blue ley essence glowing within. The gates slammed shut in seconds, or the longer lasting ones proved too small to be of any use.

When dawn broke, Umaq declared victory.

A shoulder-height staff having two prongs, one longer than the other, finally split the earth in a proper ley gate. All dual prongs with the same length had produced unsuccessful results. However, the idea to try different lengths on the same fork came to mind just when he wanted to quit. After additional molding and cutting, he finally accomplished his quest.

Umaq held the rod before him and struck it. The fork hummed in double rich tones felt in his chest. A gate half the length of the room yawned open, the world's blue spirit shining inside. He counted forty seconds before it closed. Then another test…forty-five seconds. Forty-two in the third trial. Following several more attempts, the average opening lasted just under forty-five seconds and the average size remained the same.

"Long and large enough for whatever I desire," he said in a dry, raspy voice.

Exhaustion, hunger, and dehydration robbed him of a thrilling and energetic victory lap. Instead, he collapsed on the ground as the ley staff rested in his arms. Frightening and confusing dreams plagued a restless sleep. He struggled to wake up and escape senseless nightmares. He eventually stirred and the cold, hard ground greeted him by inflicting aches all over his body.

Umaq moaned and sat up. Pain flared in his joints and muscles. His back screamed from working all night. The mere act of standing winded him. Holding the staff, he shuffled out of the fallen temple and headed for the steps leading down into the Sacred Plaza. The low morning sun meant he had only slept a few hours past dawn.

At the top step, Machu Picchu lay silent below him as most of the demons retreated into their burrows. Across the grass of the Central Plaza, only two witches walked on a stone path. The citadel appeared gorgeous in the early sun, a shiny gem on the mountaintop beneath fluffy white clouds and a brilliant blue sky. The cold air felt crisp and clean against Umaq's skin, fresh and revitalizing as he took a deep breath.

Feeling better, he descended into the Sacred Plaza. He should have headed straight to his chambers for rest, but instead paused near the Temple of the Three Windows to study the ley staff gripped in his hand. Should he ride the wave of success and begin trials for another project he'd had in mind these past few days? After a few moments, Umaq nodded. No rest for the wicked is how the saying went.

He stepped into the temple and opened the large wooden coffer near the windows. He placed the ley staff inside and moved some of the old demon bones around.

Finding the black dagger used to kill Inti, he withdrew the weapon and inspected it in front of the inactive demon portal.

Since the day of the sun god's fall, Umaq had written copious notes of the entire experience. The preparation, type of spells involved, ingredients, side effects, unexpected events, and results. The cold, black essence he had ripped from the netherworld to bind Inti to the altar had consumed most of Umaq's effort. He had drawn a massive amount of darkness from across the planes, and it had nearly broken him. But with smaller, controlled doses, that raw power had potential for other uses. Instead of releasing that force…it could be absorbed.

Umaq launched into another round of hard work. He dove into his notes and a set of tomes to search for information and spells. He ran back and forth between the temple and his home to collect items, then began to complete tasks. A circle of black candles spread before the Uku-Pacha window. Ground jaguar bone lay sprinkled on the stone sill. He removed his shirt and drew dark symbols on his chest and arms using a piece of charcoal. Demon teeth clattered on the stone tile as he dumped several inside the circle.

Arrangements complete, Umaq held the black dagger and stepped into the ring of candles. He took several calming breaths and placed the edge of the blade against his opposite forearm. With the portal dormant, the view through the window showed the grassy Central Plaza and the stone structures beyond. Anxiety quickened his heart and tension froze him in place. He set his feet apart, a slight bend in his knees. A drop of sweat trickled down his left temple.

Minutes passed. The portal's random activations meant he could be standing here for fifteen minutes or a couple hours. But he had already prepared. His mind and body stood ready to accept whatever rushed out of the gateway—ultimate power or death.

Umaq had no idea how long he stood there before the portal flashed to life. The window view suddenly switched to a black, rocky landscape topped by a purple sky. Heat from the nether realm wafted into the cool air of the temple. In the far distance, something with great wings and a long tail flew in the violet sky.

Umaq shouted an enchantment in a demonic tongue. "*Blood spills, an offer given. A sacrifice flows, through my will I have striven. My soul may burn and my body fall to its grave, a chance I take for the black essence I crave!*"

He drew the blade across his arm and opened a deep cut. Blood flew toward the portal and into the demon realm in a steady stream. After a few moments, the blood flow increased and would not abate. Umaq panicked. The dagger clattered on the floor as he clamped a hand over the cut. Blood oozed between his fingers and slid beneath his palm. More of his lifeforce rushed through the gateway. Vertigo and weakness dropped to him to his knees in a near faint.

Struggling to remain conscious, he saw a black cloud form on the other side of the portal. The dark mass approached and sailed through the opening just as the blood flow halted. The black essence flowed into the wound on his arm, and he screamed in pain. His body burned as if engulfed by flame. His flesh throbbed from a thousand cuts. He fell and writhed in agony, eyes squeezed shut. Candles spun and rolled across the floor, scattered by his thrashing feet.

"Umaq!"

Someone's hand tried to steady him. Breathing hard, he rose to a sitting position and found Cessani crouched at his side.

"What in the world is going on?" she asked, her wide eyes glancing around the temple room. "Your setup…this is some really dark magic, Umaq. What have you done?"

"I'm fine, thanks for asking," he said, climbing to his feet.

He felt a lot more than fine. Reborn. Elated. The black nether essence coursed inside him after a successful ritual. The process had nearly killed him, but that no longer mattered. The wound on his arm sealed. Newfound strength—both mystical and physical—vibrated his bones and muscles. Dormant spaces in his mind had awoken with untapped knowledge and capability. The environment communicated to him in ways he never imagined. The air revealed spiritual secrets. The earth beneath his feet shared its hidden wisdom. The stonework and life around him, human or otherwise, became part of this shared insight of the world.

"Umaq, your eyes!" Cessani exclaimed. They're turning black."

"Are they?" he asked absently.

A mirror would verify if the ugly yellow filling his eye sockets had gone black, but his vision suddenly sharpened. He looked through the Uku-Pacha window, the portal now latent again. Outside in the morning light, everything in his view lay crystal clear. Colors, contours, and texture leapt out in great detail. He observed rough scales on distant demons napping in the shade of a wall, and their cracked and chipped horns. The blades of grass in the Central Plaza appeared as if he could touch them, each one crisp and moist in the early morning while insects crawled in-between.

His scalp began to prickle. He ran fingers through his hair, and clumps of it fell out. Cessani gaped at him, but Umaq laughed. "I suppose a change in eye color and hair loss are a small price to pay for my new power. I've absorbed the essence of the netherworld into my body, Cessani. I have so much to research, and my potential is unlimited."

"You don't realize how dangerous this is," the old witch stated. "You've already achieved triumph over Inti. Our plan succeeded, and the new era will begin. What more do you want?"

"To be a god," he said simply. "The portal must open permanently so I can control both realms and unite them. But to do that, I need to further darken this plane by destroying another sun deity. I'm thinking Helios in Athens." He smiled. "Feel like taking a road trip?"

Cessani shook her head, her face pale as she stepped back in horror. "You've lost your mind, Umaq. This has gone too far! The fall of another sun god will completely destroy nature's balance. Mystical energy will grow unstable and the consequences severe. And the demons already here are sufficient. This mortal realm cannot endure a massive infestation under so much darkness. I will have no part in this, and neither will the moon goddesses."

"I expected this reaction, but I'm not worried," said Umaq. "I am more than capable of handling this myself."

"Please be reasonable," Cessani implored. "I received word from Salem that Grace and her coven have started an uprising. We should concentrate on holding the city as our base of operations outside of Machu Picchu. Come with me. I think time away from here will do you some good."

"Witch affairs are your concern, my dear," he replied. "I will remain here to test my new abilities. And by the way, I figured out how to open a ley gate. All that's left is to learn how to travel. We witnessed the disaster for Sybil during her attempt. When I master ley line use, I'll be able to move my demon army around the world in an instant. After the destruction of another sun god, Sybil and Marcelo won't have anywhere to run."

He held up his hands. Black, misty essence rose from each fingertip in smoky tendrils. "Killing them will be too easy," he continued. "Instead, I'll renew my original plan from Salem and force the vampire and witch under my control. Marcelo will drink Sybil dry and infect her with his demonic essence. After she falls deep under my command, my old experiments using demonic hybrids—like with Marcelo five hundred years ago—will continue."

"Stop this madness right now," Cessani warned. "Come back to your senses."

Umaq laughed. Black mist continued to issue from his fingers. After rising overhead, the dark cloud floated down and covered his entire frame. "Are you going to stop me? I don't think so. Go enjoy your witch rule, and let me be."

Wrapped in dark essence, Umaq closed his eyes and envisioned his home. He saw himself standing in his room, the bed unmade and his writings scattered across the desk. A plate of unfinished food sat on the small table. His coat hung on a wooden peg. The frayed brown rug…

He opened his eyes and grinned at familiar surroundings. The teleportation worked! The smoky mass had transported him from the temple to his chambers. He wished he could witness the look on Cessani's face. Instinct and effort using the previously unexplored spaces in his mind had brought success. Excitement filled him, and he couldn't wait to see how much more he could accomplish.

Umaq finished the rest of the stale food on the dish, then finally laid down to sleep.

Chapter Eleven

The Head of the Snake

In her driveway, Grace shoved the last suitcase into the trunk of her car. Nothing else fit. Boxes, kitchen appliances, and garbage bags filled with clothes also packed the backseat. She closed the trunk and faced one of Cessani's red-robed goons. "Are you satisfied? My whole life is crammed into the car. You got what you wanted, and I'm leaving."

"Over the past few days, your coven put on quite a show with humorous street protests and even a tiny riot," the man said. "Your efforts were quickly squashed, but we won't be satisfied until you're far away from Salem."

Grace checked the time on her phone—almost nine o'clock at night. "Where is Cessani's lapdog, the necromancer Nastasiya? She's in charge of the city now while Cessani is gone. I thought she'd be the one escorting me out of town, just to rub it in."

The man smiled within the shadows of the hood. "Oh, you'll meet with Nastasiya one last time. She's at the checkpoint on the corner of Washington Square and Brown Street in front of the former Salem Witch Museum. She will have some further instructions for you."

"Further instructions?" Grace asked in anger. "Is disbanding my coven and kicking me out of town not enough?"

"You'd better hurry, she's expecting you," the man replied, folding his arms. "And you're lucky Cessani isn't here to see you out herself. I know she would have enjoyed that very much."

"At least I won't have to see your ugly face anymore," Grace said bitterly as she opened the car door.

The male witch blocked the door as Grace tried to close it. "Take the highway to Lafayette Street. Stop at each checkpoint. None of us will rest until your taillights are on the road to Boston to catch your flight."

Grace smiled. "I'll play nice and do as you say. Now get your greasy sausage fingers off my door so I can leave."

She slammed the door shut. The red-robed man tensed as if he might demand to ride with her, which is what Grace feared. She exhaled in relief when he remained in the yard as she pulled out of the driveway.

Grace briefly looked up at the night sky. Days ago, she had sensed the drastic change in nature after the sun god's destruction. The unexpected shock had dropped her to the floor in her kitchen. Panic froze her blood and she had cried, not just for the dangerous repercussions to the mystical environment, but more for Sybil and Marcelo's fate when phone calls went unanswered. Where were her beloved friends? Were they all right following Umaq's victory?

With Salem and the surrounding area in chaos, Grace had plenty of distractions and responsibility to continue the fight at home. Cessani's coven had taken advantage of the sun god's demise to quickly—and sometimes violently—enforce witch rule in Salem and neighboring cities like Marblehead and Peabody. The Salem Witch Museum had ironically been converted into the coven's headquarters. Helpless to stand against the witches' newfound power, the mayor, city council, and police had been stripped of all authority.

The checkpoints throughout the city served as physical and mental reminders of who called the shots. Magical barriers and several un-manned defenses also surrounded the city through a method of control and protection. Night and day, Nastasiya's risen undead patrolled the neighborhoods using fear as the greatest weapon to subdue the innocent civilians. The streets remained mostly deserted as confused and frightened residents tried to cope with this abrupt change in their lives.

Elsewhere, news reports spoke of the witch uprisings in Boston and other large metropolises like New York and Los Angeles. Even Beijing, Moscow, and London started to see violence and increased supernatural activity. Paranormal beings of all kinds appeared in greater numbers, many of them siding with Cessani. Other creatures remained neutral; however, they also took advantage of the mystical imbalance and broke from "normal mortal society" to act out and behave as they wished.

Cessani's coven might be content in this new era, yet Grace understood that the witch revolution represented a mere sideshow of the real threat from Umaq. The demon summoner and portal master would not have gone through all this trouble just to have witches running around in charge. Someone like him desired far greater things. She had witnessed part of his terrible ambition when he kidnapped dear Sybil, then bewitched Marcelo to take her life and convert her into an undead. That effort had failed, but snuffing the light of a sun god had not.

Grace left her neighborhood and turned onto the highway. "I'll be at every checkpoint, don't you worry about that," she said to herself while setting up the hands-free device to call Ben and Elisa from her coven.

"Grace, is everything all right?" Ben's voice asked through the speaker.

"Our nice fake protests and riot worked," she answered. "After quelling our rebellion, they still think I've given up and am leaving. But we'll have to modify our plan tonight. Nastasiya wasn't at my house like I expected. She's stationed in front of the museum, so we'll have to attack her right in the serpent's nest."

"Cutting the head off the snake is never easy," Ben replied. "I'll group text the others and let them know. Are we still on for the checkpoints? Elisa and I are sitting in the truck, ready to rock."

"Yes, that part has not changed," said Grace. "I'm heading for Lafayette now. I'll be at the first checkpoint by Salem State University in a minute." She took a deep breath and tried to keep the nervous tremor out of her voice. "This is it, Ben. No turning back once we start."

"Elisa and I are always with you," Ben stated. "Everyone else is also ready and at their respective locations. No one has backed out or is having second thoughts. We can do this, Grace."

She wiped a tear from her eye, glad her friends couldn't see through the phone line. "I see red robes ahead by the intersection, the first stop. It's showtime."

Grace slowed the Prius in front of a wooden barrier stretched across the highway. Two robed witches and an animated corpse manned this station. The undead creature stood in the center of the road, its hood down to reveal a half-rotted bald head. It only had one eye. A knot of pink worms squirmed on its right shoulder. A thick spiderweb covered its left ear. Grace lowered the window as one of the witches approached.

"Good riddance, traitor," a woman said. "You are no witch. May the Maiden and Mama Quilla spit in your face as you leave."

Grace glanced south on Lafayette and spotted headlights approaching—Ben's large truck. Her heart hammered in anticipation, and sweat from her palms moistened the steering wheel.

"Thank you for that lovely visual," she said, her throat dry.

"Hey, there's a vehicle coming," the other male witch called out.

"Halt them over at the crossroads," the woman ordered. "I'm not done with Grace yet."

The resurrected corpse made choking sounds in its throat. It pointed at Grace, then at Ben's truck.

"Keep that zombie still!" the woman shouted at the man. "This night is too important to screw up."

The male witch approached the truck idling across the way. Tires suddenly barked on the asphalt, and the truck shot forward. The man shouted in alarm and scrambled out of the way. Engine revving, Ben maneuvered the big vehicle toward the undead and smashed it in a powerful impact. Large tires crushed the creature as it rolled beneath the chassis and left behind a mess on the pavement.

Grace pulled the handle of the door and shoved it open using both feet. The door struck the female witch, and she fell. Grace flew out of the Prius and launched a fire spell at the bottom of the woman's robe. The witch screamed and ripped off the smoldering garment. Half-naked, she tried to run toward the university, but Elisa climbed out of the truck and knocked the witch unconscious using a wooden post.

The male witch appeared too shocked to react. Pale, he raised his hands in surrender. "I…wh-what is this?" he stammered. "Don't…please don't hurt me!"

"It's too late," Ben said, stepping out of the vehicle.

He threw orange dust into the man's face. The sleep-inducing powder dropped the witch to the ground. Ben dragged the man off the road and laid him next to the woman on the university lawn. He bound both their hands and feet with cord. Elisa found their phones and smashed them to bits.

Grace and her friends formed a tight hug in the middle of the highway. Her phone buzzed, and she checked the message. "Patty's group did it! Another checkpoint destroyed by the gas station on Ocean Avenue. Two zombies dead and Cessani's witches incapacitated."

"Our plan is working," Elisa said in excitement. "Clearing the streets of the undead will severely impact Nastasiya's hold on Salem. Those witches aren't so tough without their corpse bodyguards around. And after we take down the necromancer, there'll be no more zombies at all. The source of the city's fear will be gone."

"The night is young," Grace said, worried. "I'll feel better after hearing positive results from the other groups. Let's move on to the next checkpoint. You know the drill."

Leaving the scene, Grace drove around the barrier and turned north on Lafayette as Ben trailed behind. No time to cover their tracks or hide evidence. The goal was to hit Cessani's followers hard and fast, all in one night from different locations. Grace's coven had stretched thin across the city, each small group coordinating their attacks. Catching the enemy by surprise remained critical, as a prolonged confrontation would be dangerous.

The phone buzzed again. She sighed in relief as a group text from Robert reported another successful raid. More streets had been cleared…and the path to Nastasiya grew shorter. A moment later, a familiar car honked from the side of the road and fell into line behind Ben to form a caravan. That would be Patty and her brothers after their fruitful encounter.

Grace approached a crossroads and watched her rearview mirror as Ben and Patty's vehicles turned off the highway in opposite directions, as they planned. Continuing alone, she slowed at the next checkpoint where Lafayette met Derby Street next to Howling Wolf Taqueria. Another group of witches and zombies patrolled the area.

A robed man holding a smartphone pressed to his ear approached her open window. He looked at Grace, frowned at the screen in his hand, then tapped a button and slipped the device into a pocket. "The squad at the university was supposed to call when you were on the way. But whatever, you are here now. Stay inside."

The man walked slowly around her car and looked through the windows. Was this some kind of inspection? Grace nervously drummed her fingers on the steering wheel. Her eyes darted left and right along Derby Street. Any moment now.

The man completed his round and returned to the driver's side window. "So, you finally admitted defeat," he boasted. "It seems—"

"Yes, yes, blah, blah!" Grace said loudly. She grew tired of every witch in the city giving her a little speech on the way out. But to kill time, she should have let him continue, since Ben and Patty hadn't arrived yet. "You've won. What's in it for you? What has Cessani promised that's so great?"

The intersection exploded in action. Two cars barreled into view from the left and right on Derby. Tires screeched, and wooden barriers shattered into splinters. The man started to run toward the bedlam, but Grace stepped on the accelerator and jerked the wheel to the left. The front of the car cut off the man's sprint, and he tumbled over the hood. Grace climbed out and gripped the top of his head, then sent an electric shock into his skull to knock him out.

She dove back behind the wheel. The car sped over broken pieces of wood until it plowed into and over a risen corpse. The vehicle bounced as it crushed the monster into the asphalt. Grace stopped the car and flew out to assist Ben, Elisa, and the others. The element of surprise and the multi-sided attack worked. Three undead became dead once again, and four witches lay still with zip ties around their wrists and ankles.

A vehicle with a cracked windshield approached and flashed its headlights in a recognized pattern. "It's Robert and his crew!" Grace said in relief.

The minivan stopped in the intersection and Robert poked his head out the driver's side window. "All of North Shore Medical Campus is clear." A bloody bandage wrapped his forehead. "Looks like we missed the fun here."

Concerned, Grace walked over and cupped Robert's face while inspecting the injured area. "Are you all right? Your group has been amazing, but you need to sit the next one out."

"No way, the next one is the last and most important," he said. "Courtney is in the back seat with a sprained ankle and Jacob has a broken thumb, but the fools refuse to stop now. Time is our enemy. Let's finish this, Grace. I have a feeling the citizens of Salem will rise up once Nastasiya is out of the picture."

Time is our enemy. Grace and her coven could defeat witches and monsters all evening, but time remained the unstoppable foe. If their mission didn't continue tonight—as in right now—another opportunity would never arrive. Cessani's coven would grow stronger and more prepared.

"Let's move!" she called to the others. "You know your routes on the way to the museum, and you've memorized the plan. Wait for my text." She hurried back to the car and drove toward the witches' headquarters at the former Salem Witch Museum.

Heart thundering, Grace turned right on Derby then left on Hawthorne Boulevard. She wished she had taken a moment to tell her coven how proud she felt and how much she loved them. Pivotal moments like these required some words of encouragement and camaraderie. Everyone had already displayed their enthusiasm and devotion; however, Grace would have enjoyed a minute to share those emotions with her friends.

Nearing the museum, she took several deep breaths and struggled to calm down. Her breathing technique did little to quiet her nerves as she passed the Hawthorne Hotel. The trees and green grass of Salem Common came into view just past the hotel. She rolled to a stop at the intersection of Brown Street and gasped in shock.

Witches, risen corpses, and a horde of other creatures packed the area in front of the Salem Witch Museum. The action resembled a raucous Halloween block party. Black, brown, and gray-haired werewolves howled and shoved each other. Grotesque ghouls with gangling limbs and slick diseased skin nibbled on meaty bones. Translucent, wailing banshees wearing billowing gowns floated among the throng. A dozen toothy imps hopped about in loud, guttural chatter. Tall, horned demons—more than likely some of Umaq's stock—moved in cautious gaits as if anticipating an attack. Adding to the jaw-dropping scene, a group of vampires stood calm and aloof in their own cluster.

And standing by the curb in the center of the unexpected party, Nastasiya smiled at Grace and motioned her over.

Terror froze Grace's blood. Her bones melted into jelly, and her muscles grew limp. Somehow, a trembling hand crept to the phone and frantic thumbs texted one word to her friends over and over.

ABORT. ABORT. ABORT.

The quest for Grace's coven had ended. Her courage and determination vanished in the reality of the situation before her. Where on earth had all these creatures come from? And most importantly, why were they here? Days of planning and collecting intelligence did not reveal any hint of this sudden Halloween-fest. Grace's strategy to liberate Salem now seemed foolish and arrogant. Did she really think it would all be so simple?

But despite the failure, she remained in control of one thing—saving the lives of her beloved companions. Every good plan had a failsafe for escape, and she had been adamant with her coven about immediately pulling back should something go wrong. No questions. No hesitation. Just retreat and go home. She felt confident her friends would obey the command to abort. Knowing they would be safe provided Grace with enough bravery for one final act.

Some of the monsters surrounded her car in a cacophony of howls, shouts, and growls. Claws raked across the hood. Fists beat on the roof. Strong hands rocked the Prius back and forth. Grace ignored the show of force and fixed her gaze on Nastasiya. Slowly, she drove forward through the intersection as the monsters parted to let her through. She turned left and parked against the curb directly in front of the museum.

A parched throat wouldn't let Grace swallow. Even her palms felt dry, as if fear had sweated the last drop from her tense body. Her heart beat so fast she wondered if cardiac arrest would stop her from exiting the vehicle. But on she went, unbuckling the seatbelt and opening the door to step out.

The banshees wailed louder. The werewolves cried out to the dark sky. Ghouls leapt about like frogs and clicked their teeth. The smaller imps danced and flapped leathery wings. The silent vampires watched with stoic expressions.

Nastasiya's malicious smile didn't abate as Grace walked around the front of her car toward the necromancer. Her mind grew more distant from her surroundings. In the background, the medieval castle architecture of the Salem Witch Museum, with is brown brick and frontal towers, disappeared from view. The monsters and all the ruckus went away. Her focus remained only on Nastasiya as she approached.

"Welcome to the celebration," the necromancer said. "You're just in time."

"All of this just for me?" Grace asked. "I'm flattered you went to such extremes to see me off."

"Oh, the celebration is not for you," Nastasiya replied. "But your departure coincides with a special arrival."

Grace ignored the announcement and pomp. She took a moment to bathe in enormous relief as no squealing tires or racing engines sounded. Her friends had obeyed the urgent message to terminate. Intense gratification released tension from her body, and she could finally complete tonight's mission.

Grace slipped a hand into a pocket and gripped the hardened clay knife inside. She had fashioned the weapon using the special sand purchased from the Crow Haven Corner. The grains had been soaked by the blood of thousands of soldiers from terrible wars in different parts of the world. The enchantment on the blade would place the victim in a coma. Just a nick would put Nastasiya down for at least a year.

Stepping forward, she plunged the weapon into Nastasiya's shoulder...or at least she thought she did.

The blade turned into sand, and only her fist thumped against the necromancer's arm. Grace stared at her hand in disbelief as the grains slipped between her fingers and fell to the street.

Nastasiya froze and returned an equal look of shock. She then punched Grace and sent her crashing to the pavement.

The surrounding creatures bellowed. Red-robed witches yanked Grace by the hair and clothes to lift her. Seized in their grip, she stood on wobbly legs and glanced around as the throng suddenly grew quiet.

"Good thing I was here to stop that knife," a female voice called.

Creatures parted in front of the museum, and Grace stared in astonishment. The Maiden, Goddess of the Moon, stood on the sidewalk. A red robe draped over the young deity with a silver waxing moon pinned to her left shoulder. Tiny sparkles of lunar light radiated in her waist-length white hair. Despite the grave circumstances, a playful spirit and humor glittered in her teal eyes.

Nastasiya bowed to the Maiden. "I am forever in your debt, dear Goddess. You saved me."

"The knife was easy," said the Maiden. "But those greasy potato chips you enjoy will be the death of you, Nastasiya. Nothing I can do for you there." She approached Grace and patted her cheek. "Poor, sweet Grace. You must be so confused while worshipping the Moon Goddesses and having me break from tradition. What shall we do with you?"

"Some time in confinement should clear her head," Cessani's voice announced behind the throng. The old witch had stepped out of the museum to join the Maiden on the sidewalk. "Grace rejected our kind offer to simply leave Salem and then tried to harm Nastasiya. The woman is too much of a liability to be on the loose, here or elsewhere. She'll be locked up inside our headquarters."

"That's fine with me, it's your house after all," the Maiden responded, inspecting her nails.

"I thought you were in Machu Picchu," Grace said to Cessani, undeterred by the dire threat of imprisonment. At least they hadn't thrown her to the wolves—literally. "As Umaq's puppet, shouldn't you be with him in Peru?"

"I returned to ensure you were dealt with, and it appears this episode is over," Cessani answered. "Take her inside," she commanded the witches.

Grace struggled in vain as the escort shoved her inside the building. To her surprise, the interior of the Salem Witch Museum headed toward a complete transformation. The name no longer applied as new construction, decor, offices, and conference rooms had replaced the witch trial scenes and other spaces. Some areas appeared newly finished. Other sections had hanging plastic, sheets of drywall, covered furniture, cans of paint, and tools lying about. Overall, the environment gave the impression of a professional governing office. It showed just how serious Cessani had been about establishing control.

Down a hallway, Grace found herself in an empty room that more than likely used to serve as storage. The witches didn't bother closing the door. Instead, they cast an invisible hex over the open doorway, which held no matter how hard she tried to break free.

Alone, Grace hoped her coven remained in their homes and would refrain from looking for her. She also thought of Sybil and Marcelo. Deep worry lifted her shoulders in a sigh.

"Please be safe, my friends," she whispered.

Chapter Twelve

Wolf in Wolf's Clothing

In the Broad Street Cemetery in Salem, Sybil and Johann crouched behind a large headstone after the Mother had transported them into the city late at night. Several rows ahead in the line of graves, a cluster of hungry ghouls feasted on bones and decaying flesh ripped from the tombs. In another part of the cemetery, a single banshee hovered over a fresh plot and opened her mouth in a high-pitched moan.

"What in the hell is going on here?" Johann whispered. "Strange creatures are all over the city. I'm one of them, but I didn't expect so many."

"The supernatural world hath been roused by the sun god's fall, I warrant," Sybil replied. "The darkening of yonder mystical energy hath disquieted their minds." She gazed at him in concern. "Thereof, how do you fare forthwith?"

Johann pressed a hand to his left temple. "I have a headache, to be honest. And I can't stop sweating."

Sybil worried over her friend's condition. Bringing him here had been a gamble, but after seeing all these beasts and spirits running around, she welcomed his assistance. "If you desire to rest, we shall seek a better place to hide, lest you fall ill."

"Let's keep going," he said, his expression determined. "Hopefully we'll find your friend soon."

Sybil had tried calling Grace several times, but her friend's phone seemed to be off. Afraid to find out why, she left the cemetery with Johann and led the way down Broad Street. The silence from the neighborhood unsettled her. After the Mother mentioned Grace had faced adversity in Salem, Sybil expected some sort of commotion in the streets. Except for the monsters, not a soul moved and nearly all the houses appeared dark. No TVs or radios could be heard from the surrounding neighborhood, and no cars drove about.

She turned left on Summer Street and halted in the darkness beneath a tree. In the intersection ahead, several vehicles and red-robed individuals stood in the roundabout. Sybil motioned to Johann. The pair moved closer and took cover between two homes along the sidewalk. She peeked around the corner of the house to study the odd scene.

A sprawling mess covered the street. Broken pieces of wood, torn clothing, shattered glass, an overturned car, and bodies littered the area. A robed male knelt by three unconscious people and used a blade to remove bindings from their wrists and ankles. He then waved a hand over their faces, and the prone individuals stirred.

"Looks like a battle raged here not too long ago," Johann said softly. "Those robes match the witches' attire in news footage from Machu Picchu. Definitely Cessani's crew."

"Other bodies lie in yonder street, but that man is ignoring them," Sybil observed. "I fear the violence hath taken some lives."

Johann stifled a laugh. "Those bodies, my dear Sybil, were dead long before they were killed again, if that makes sense. My canine nose can smell those rotted, resurrected corpses from here. We call them zombies. When this is all over, ask Marcelo to show you a good zombie movie. I recommend *Train to Buson*."

Relieved knowing people hadn't died in the street, Sybil grew even more concerned about Grace. "I warrant this battle hath involved Grace's coven, 'twas what the Mother warned me of. My heart wonders if she hath striven all over the city."

"Let's find out," Johann said as the pair slipped away in the opposite direction.

Over the next couple hours, they confirmed the widespread destruction of battle across Salem. Several outposts had been attacked and left similar results of the chaos on Summer Street. Cessani's witches had begun the process of rebuilding the makeshift checkpoints and doubling the watch. Throughout the once quiet streets, pickup trucks packed with red-robed coven members now roamed across the area. The remaining zombies had been placed on guard as well. Sybil and Johann completed the investigation at Grace's empty house in the southern part of the city.

"She hath not come hither," Sybil said in distress. She stood on Grace's lawn and glanced around the silent neighborhood. "I feel faint with worry. Do you believe someone had a fair sight of her?"

"He might know," Johann said, nodding toward a house across the street. "Someone's been watching us from the porch shadows. I can smell their sweat and fear, not exactly the scent of an enemy."

Sybil couldn't see anyone, but she stepped into the street and waved toward the house. A moment later, an elderly man emerged and cautiously approached.

"You're not wearing red robes, so I hope you won't attack me," the man said. "My name is Stanley. Why are you at Grace's house?"

"We are friends," said Sybil. "I received word that trouble hath found Grace, thus my companion and I arrived hither. Are you perhaps conversant with her whereabouts?"

"I'm afraid you're too late," Stanley replied. "I'm not in her coven, but we've been neighbors for fifteen years and I know most of the members." Anguish overcame his features as he shook his head. "Grace started a street war tonight, the brave girl. She was captured and is being held in the new witch headquarters at the Salem Witch Museum. Cessani has returned and she's not alone. A deity is with her, a goddess of the moon! Not to mention a circus of monsters and ghosts have appeared out of nowhere."

"Hey, I resemble that circus," Johann said. "Werewolf here."

"Well, those are all over the city, too," Stanley replied. "And from what I hear they've been acting strangely. Dangerous, even."

Sybil closed her eyes and took a deep breath. She wanted to scream in frustration and cry. Grace…a prisoner! The courageous and passionate woman had fought to liberate the city. And now Cessani appeared with a moon deity at her side. No matter. Sybil would do anything to save her friend and continue the war after losing the first battle to Umaq.

"No need to say anything," Johann said to Sybil. "Your face says it all, woman." He pumped a fist. "Let's go rescue Grace!"

"I wish I could go with you," said Stanley. "But this old veteran's fighting days are long past. I'll drive you as close to downtown as possible while avoiding red robes. We'll head far west, then cut back toward the city through Peabody."

Not wanting to waste any time, Sybil agreed. On the way, Stanley proved to be an excellent accomplice using his military background. His knowledge of the highways, layout of the city, and lesser-known side streets allowed the car to penetrate close to downtown without being detected by physical or magical defenses. He had also grown accustomed to how Cessani's witches operated. As he explained, the coven's pattern of movement, their numbers, and shift changes were subjects he had become familiar with.

The car crept past the Flint Street bridge and stopped on the corner of Federal Street next to St. James Church. After waiting a few minutes, Stanley checked his watch, then suddenly turned left and sped through a neighborhood. He finally slowed at Murphy's Funeral Home and maneuvered the car in the shadows close to the side of the building.

He pointed through the windshield. "Salem District Court buildings are across the way. From there, the Salem Witch Museum is a straight shot east. Good luck, and be careful."

Sybil turned in the passenger seat and took his hand between hers. "Truly, I thank you with all my heart, kind sir. I shall be certain to make Grace conversant about your assistance and bravery hitherto. Farewell."

Sybil and Johann hopped out of the car. Crouched behind a tree, they waited until a truck full of red-robed witches drove by before crossing North Street in a run. The pair hurried into the court complex and halted in the darkness beside the Essex County Superior Court.

She gestured toward the street. "I warrant we can—"

At a nearby distance, a piercing wolf howl reverberated in the night. Another howl answered farther away, followed by a third and a fourth much closer. The eerie calls seemed to blast over the entire city—wails of pain or excitement, torment or ecstasy. Sybil couldn't tell the difference, but the emotional shrieks raised gooseflesh on her skin.

Johann collapsed at her side. He trembled on knees and elbows, head buried beneath his hands.

"Shut the hell up!" he screamed.

"Johann," Sybil said in alarm. She placed her hand on his curved back, but he pushed her away.

"Those stupid hairy beasts don't know how to handle their liquor," he said, laughing.

Johann stood and glared at the dark sky. He cupped his hands around his mouth and shouted, "It's just some extra moon juice, you idiots! Have some decency!"

Panicked, Sybil glanced up and down the street hoping no one had heard. She looked back at Johann and realized he had to remain here. Apparently, her werewolf friend couldn't handle his liquor, either.

"You speak true, Johann, yonder moon is at fault," she said. "And aforesaid, the lunar goddess's presence in town worsens the ailment, I warrant. Please remaineth hither. I shall go forth to inspect yonder area ahead."

Thick blond hair began to grow from Johann's cheeks and forearms. His dark eyes turned glassy and distant. The nails on his hands elongated.

"Sybil," he panted, shoulders and chest heaving. "You really need to run away from me...now!"

He threw his garments off right before he increased in size. Hair now covered his entire body. His head and face transformed into the snarling muzzle of a wolf.

Sybil turned and dashed into the street. Johann's paws pounded the asphalt just behind her. Without stopping, she summoned the miniature lighting over her body and teleported onto the roof of the neighboring Essex Probate and Family Court facility.

"Johann, please stop!" she called down to him.

The werewolf looked up, hatred in its gaze. His tongue lolled, and saliva wet the sidewalk. The beast leapt at the wall. Claws tore into the side of the building as he quickly scaled it. Sybil jumped off the roof. A strong pocket of wind engulfed her and slowed the fall until her feet touched the asphalt. She crossed Federal Street and sprinted into the wide parking lot of the Tabernacle Congregational Church.

The fast, agile werewolf bounded in pursuit. Approaching the back entry of the church, Sybil thrust out a palm and sent a hardened block of air toward the doors. The transparent block obliterated the doorway and sent wood shards flying. She ran into the building and away from Johann's savage roar a short distance behind.

Hurrying down the aisle in the main area of worship, Sybil extended her arms to the side. Pews slid across the tile floor and flipped over in haphazard directions to try and slow Johann down. The powerful werewolf smashed through the obstacle course. White stuffing from seats and bench splinters flew in a whirlwind driven by the wolf's flailing limbs and sharp claws.

Sybil blasted through the front doors of the church and ran onto Washington Street. She couldn't maintain this chase forever; Johann would certainly catch her. She also didn't want to fight her friend. For both of their safeties, she needed to get far enough away to reassess the situation and provide help for him.

The werewolf's claws clicked on the pavement in a mad hunt. Out of nowhere, something collided against Sybil and knocked the air from her lungs. She found herself in someone's ice-cold arms, her face pressed against a shoulder as the individual moved with incredible speed. The pace and sudden change of direction dizzied her. The surroundings zipped by in a roar of freezing wind. Fear of falling kept her arms wrapped around the person's neck, although her skin began to burn from the intense cold.

The sensation of speed finally stopped and left her breathless. "Marcelo?" Sybil managed to ask as the world spun. Woozy, she nearly fell when the arms released her. Her heart quickened as she looked up in anticipation.

An Asian woman returned the stare. Having a short stature, her flawless light skin nearly glowed in the night. A thick braid, black as the sky, hung in front of a shoulder down to her stomach. A glittering choker adorned her slender neck, matching bracelets on each wrist. A red blouse pattered with white flowers topped a pair of skinny jeans torn at both knees. Black polish glistened on the nails of her bare feet and hands.

Sybil and the woman stood high on the roof of a parking garage. The court buildings where she had hidden earlier with Johann lay across the street. A wolf howled somewhere in the city, but she couldn't be certain it originated from Johann.

"Marcelo?" the stranger asked. "That handsome Spaniard is not here. Although, I'm certain he will be soon."

Sybil gazed toward the woman—a vampire. An immense aura surrounded the undead, a powerful outward pressure that seemed to *dent* the air. Sybil hadn't felt the aura while carried, but now the sudden pressure forced her to step back as if an invisible hand pushed her chest. The fierce cold from before also wafted from the woman and bit Sybil's skin. Wrapping arms around herself in a shiver, she had never met or even heard of a vampire such as this one.

"Who are you?" Sybil asked in state of awe, momentarily forgetting about Marcelo.

"My name is Daiyu, which means black jade." The woman smiled. "It's Chinese, in case you were wondering. And you must be Sybil, the time-traveling witch."

"How are you conversant of me?" she asked in surprise. "And of Marcelo?"

Daiyu ignored the questions and nodded toward the street. "Your furry pursuer seems to be in trouble."

Sybil glanced down the road. Johann had appeared, this time in human form, although his rage had not subsided. Naked, he screamed nonsense and tottered as if drunk. He pounded his fist against a wall and fell to his knees, sobbing.

"Johann," Sybil said in grief.

She stepped toward the edge of the roof to jump off, but an icy finger on her shoulder halted her. Sybil moved away from the frosty air and fierce pressure surrounding Daiyu. Her shoulder throbbed; the mere touch would certainly leave a bruise. "Yonder man is my friend, and he requires aid. Truly, why do you stop me?"

"There's nothing you can do for him," Daiyu replied. "Those poor devils. It's best to let them burn the intoxication out of their system. The werewolves will grow accustomed to the moon's imbalance in time. It could take days, or weeks, but your friend will be fine. If you go near him now, he may take your head off. You're lucky I saved you."

Sybil looked back at Johann. He stood on wobblily legs and disappeared around a corner.

"I do not wish for him to suffer alone," she said in tears. The vampire approached, and the air turned so cold it burned. Sybil had to again step away.

Daiyu looked surprised, then ashamed. "I'm sorry, Sybil. I wanted to put my arm around you in comfort, but I tend to forget some people can't stand to be around me. Physically, I mean." She shrugged. "And I'm sure mentally as well."

"That does sound…lonely," Sybil observed. "Though truly, I appreciate the gesture of comfort. And I am thankful to you for saving me."

"You're a sweet girl." Daiyu peered at Sybil, a look of curiosity on her face. "Marcelo is fortunate to have you."

Sybil's heart skipped as she thought of her lover recovering in bed. "If it pleases you, tell me how you are conversant about us hitherto. It would also please me to hear more about you."

Daiyu moved to the edge of the roof and gazed out over Salem. "In the movies, this is where the enigmatic figure in the night would say mysterious things to the inquiring heroine. But I've been dormant for too long, so I'll skip the suspense and get to the point.

"I'm old, Sybil. Around two thousand five-hundred years, give or take a decade. I served under China's first emperor, Qin Shi Huang, when he ordered parts of the initial Great Wall to be connected for protection of the new Qin dynasty. Am I the oldest vampire around? I don't know. Nor do I care.

"A couple weeks ago, I awoke from a twenty-year nap I had taken out of boredom. Then recently, the world changed with the sun god's destruction, and the mystical disturbance fascinates me. Gods are walking in the streets. Demons from another plane are running around, and more witches have grown in power. The supernatural world has been turned upside down, and there's much more drama to come."

Daiyu took a step forward, and Sybil retreated an equal pace. "And the time-traveling, age-defying witch is in the center of it all," the vampire continued. "Word travels fast in the supernatural realm. Who wouldn't know about you? Your journey with Marcelo began right here in Salem. You fought Umaq as he unleashed a demon infestation in this city. You tore the Earth open and rode her lifeblood across the planet. Machu Picchu has been the center of the world's attention as you continued the battle against Umaq. Even deities joined the fray. Do you believe things like that go unnoticed? It's so thrilling!"

Daiyu's face beamed in enthusiasm. The ancient vampire had mentioned the chaos fascinated her. It seemed she enjoyed talking about things that Sybil had suffered through and marked as the worst moments of her life.

"Your entertainment hath been birthed from my misery!" Sybil said in anger. "Wherein lies your part in all this? Have you sided with Cessani and Umaq?"

"I am on no one's side," Daiyu answered. "I will endure no matter what happens, as will my vampire kind." She gave Sybil a dangerous look. "As for Marcelo, he is not one of us. I know all about the demon soul leeching off him like a parasite. A soul, no matter what creature it belonged to, is unnatural and *wrong* for the undead. Marcelo shouldn't exist. He doesn't even have a group to associate with."

Terror gripped Sybil as she listened. She feared Daiyu's harsh tone and the intent behind her words.

"Marcelo is not your enemy," she said, trying to sound firm. "He hath only striven for what is right and helped many people hitherto. His existence may be different, but I warrant he is not a threat to anyone."

Daiyu laughed. "Who are you or Marcelo to judge what is right? Many people and creatures have gathered here in Salem to benefit from this new darkness. I might enjoy this new era as well, but I've been around long enough to understand that nothing lasts forever. The only thing saving you, Sybil, is the fact that I'm completely neutral. I don't care who wins, as long as it's fun to watch.

"As for Marcelo, his fate is a different matter. He has caught my attention and not in a good way. Traipsing across the planet and fighting under the guise of a true vampire does not sit well with my fellow undead. Worst of all, it was his demon soul that started this entire affair against Umaq, was it not? The old Inca tried to use Marcelo's unnatural condition to turn you into another false vampire, one filled with demonic essence and a monster Umaq could control."

"Umaq fused the demon soul to Marcelo many years agone," Sybil responded, her body tense. "'Twas a cruel experiment. Of a truth, Marcelo had no choice. Thus, he is an innocent victim."

"The process does not matter," said Daiyu. "As I mentioned before, he shouldn't even be here. The anomaly, Marcelo, will be judged…and a sentence handed down."

Sybil grew tired of Daiyu's threats and had been through too much tonight already. Her fear boiled into anger. She couldn't just tremble on the roof while Marcelo's life was in danger. Shouting in rage, she thrust out both hands and fire exploded from her palms. The blistering flames enveloped Daiyu. Sybil continued to yell as the blaze burned hotter, brighter. Thick smoke billowed into the air. The concrete edge of the building and part of the rooftop blackened.

She dropped her arms in exhaustion. Out of breath, she watched as the smoke cleared…and revealed a smiling Daiyu. The female vampire hadn't received a single burn. Not even her hair or clothes had been touched by flame.

"Whew!" Daiyu exclaimed. "That would have turned any other blood sucker into ash. Good thing I'm old and tough."

The vampire's powerful grip tightened around Sybil's left wrist. She cried out in pain as the frigid hand burned her. The enormous aura, an invisible force packed with millennia of existence, of life and death dozens of times over, pulsed around Sybil. The pressure on the air made it difficult to breathe. Dropping to her knees, she nearly swooned.

Daiyu sank her fangs into the pad of Sybil's thumb. She groaned and watched helplessly as her adversary drank. Satisfied, the undead released her grip and Sybil tumbled sideways onto the roof. She cradled her burnt wrist, the skin swollen and black as if charred by fire.

"Tasty," Daiyu said, licking her lips. "Go and speak to Cessani about your friend, Grace. Don't worry, I've put in a good word for you. Cessani's coven won't attack. This is the next act in the play, and I look forward to it." The vampire vanished in a blur of speed.

Daiyu hadn't taken much blood, but the act of being fed upon against her will made Sybil queasy. She felt violated, embarrassed at not being able to defend herself, and livid. For her burned wrist, she cast a curative spell that failed to completely heal the injury. Hissing in pain, she stood and peered out over the city.

Indecision tore at Sybil. She desired to return to Marcelo's side and remain for protection until he woke, then immediately warn him about Daiyu. She also wished to find Johann and support him through the horrid process of adjustment to the moon before he hurt anyone, or himself. Lastly, she yearned to confront

Cessani and find a way to free Grace. What path should she take? Would choosing one end in disaster for another?

For the moment, Marcelo should be safe under the moon deities' care. Johann at least had his freedom, but Grace remained a prisoner and needed help. Daiyu had arranged for Sybil to have a nonconfrontational meeting with Cessani. Going to her provided a respite from running or fighting, and Sybil realized a break is what she longed for most of all. The decision made, she leapt off the parking garage roof and summoned a gust of wind to slow her descent.

Sybil recognized the area from her previous stay in Salem. She headed east on Bridge Street, turned right on St. Peter, then left on Brown. She took her time and walked out in the open. Daiyu had spoken true; clusters of red-robed witches and zombies only stared as Sybil passed by.

An uproar greeted her when she approached the witch museum. Witches, demons, ghosts, vampires, and a variety of other night creatures swarmed the street. With Grace's wellbeing in mind, Sybil paid no attention to the commotion and marched straight through the double doors.

A pair of witches escorted her inside. Amid the new construction, she smelled fresh paint and the odor of sawed wood. Witches hurried about carrying three-ringed binders, boxes of various size, or pushing carts topped by office supplies. Other individuals sat at desks while inspecting paperwork or answering phones.

Sybil walked down a tiled hallway, and the escorts motioned her into a spacious office. Cessani sat behind a desk and typed something into a computer. The simple room lacked decoration. Paper, books, and folders lay in haphazard piles on a shelf. The furniture and carpet looked new. It appeared this office had been part of the overall museum alteration as Cessani and her coven continued to settle in.

Near the back wall, the Maiden, Goddess of the Moon, attracted Sybil's gaze. The deity lounged on a couch, pillows tucked behind her head and back. A red robe draped her lithe body. Sparkles danced in long white hair that framed a vibrant, youthful face. Teal eyes watched Sybil as the goddess ate from a small tub of ice cream.

"Sybil, please have a seat," Cessani said while looking at the monitor. She clicked the mouse a few times and continued typing.

"I have traveled hither for Grace," Sybil stated without moving. "Where does she dwell?"

"No need to be hasty, I was going to offer you coffee," Cessani replied. "I'll let you see Grace, but first we must chat." She motioned to the chair opposite the desk. "You look exhausted, and that terrible burn on your arm must hurt like heck."

Sybil glanced over to the Maiden. The deity continued to observe in silence as she licked the back of the spoon. Struggling with impatience and trying to avoid confrontation, Sybil sat in the chair and stared at Cessani.

"Good," said the old witch. "I lied about the coffee, though. We don't have anymore." She clicked the mouse again, then pushed the chair back to give Sybil her full attention. "I will set Grace free, but first you need to defeat Umaq."

Sybil gaped in disbelief. Was this yet another attempt to deceive her, as when Cessani lied about betraying Umaq and then led Sybil into the Wyman Woods to be captured?

"I know you don't trust me," Cessani continued. "But as we speak, he is planning to eliminate another sun god, this time Helios in Athens. Umaq wants to merge this realm with the demon one, and he can only accomplish that by shattering the mystical barrier between both planes and creating more darkness. Our world can survive the disappearance of one sun god, but not two. The skies would then truly darken, and unimaginable horrors would flood into existence."

Something cold pressed against Sybil's lips. She jerked her head back in surprise and tasted ice cream. Behind her, the Maiden laughed while holding the spoon. Sybil had been so focused on Cessani, she failed to notice the deity sneak up until the frozen treat touched her mouth.

"She's not lying," the Maiden said. "As a lunar deity, I'm also concerned about the darkening. Some mystical balance needs to remain. Helios' sister, the Moon Goddess Selene, must be distressed about her brother."

"But Umaq hath already attained victory after Inti's demise," Sybil said, stunned. "Truly, he achieved his goal and thus summoned forth more powerful demons. And more to your behoof, Cessani, you have established a new order. Thereof, what more could he desire?"

"Umaq has always been unstable, but this time he's gone completely mad," Cessani answered. "They say power always goes to your head. But for him, it's filled his heart, soul, and body. He's grown extremely dangerous and more powerful than ever. I caught him siphoning dark essence from the netherworld. It absorbed into his body and boosted his abilities." The old witch looked troubled. "Umaq has become a real monster, and he still wants revenge on you and Marcelo. He's out of control, and I certainly can't stop him."

"I conceive it pleases you to imprison Grace while I strive to clean up your mess," Sybil remarked in anger. "She hath nothing to do with yonder situation. Set her forth at once, and I warrant I shall stop Umaq."

"That's noble, but Grace is the only insurance I have," Cessani remarked. "And holding her hostage does please me a bit. Her rebellious coven caused quite a stir, and I need to keep them in check. I also must be certain you, Marcelo, or someone else can't come after me until this task is finished. Besides, with an endless amount of work to do, my place is here in Salem. I must govern the witches in this new era, and I can only do that in peace by knowing you're handling Umaq."

The spoonful of ice cream neared Sybil's mouth again, but this time she anticipated it. She pushed the Maiden's hand away and stood in frustration. "And what of you, dear Goddess? You have already striven against a sun god. You ought to stand against Umaq forthwith."

"I'm actually afraid of him," the deity replied between bites. "Infused by the dark essence, he's become god-like himself and has a ferocious demon army at his side. But like Cessani, Mama Quilla and I are busy doing other things. We must travel the world to guide new recruits, open other branches for the coven, and expand our influence." She smiled. "I saw you in action at

Machu Picchu. You and your talented friends are capable of facing Umaq. We leave it in your hands."

Fury shook Sybil. Cessani and the Maiden expressed concern over the perilous situation, yet chose to standby in luxury while once again, Sybil and her friends had to risk their lives. But Grace's life remained at stake as well, and the beloved woman had also sacrificed so much. Sybil would fight for her and continue to protect her friends as best as possible.

"Of a truth, my friends are not well," she said after forcing herself to calm down. "Marcelo and Salix suffer injury and ailment hitherto. The moon hath intoxicated my werewolf companion, Johann, and he roams yonder streets. I have a sundry of preparations forthwith and I cannot do this alone, I warrant."

"I have something that will help the werewolf," said the Maiden. "But before I hand it over, you must do something very important for me. It's only fair."

It didn't surprise Sybil that her adversaries continued to pitch crooked deals and blackmail. She sighed and crossed her arms. "What do you require?"

The Maiden refilled the spoon with ice cream and stepped toward Sybil. "You must have a bite."

"Do not be absurd," Sybil said, not amused.

"Then your mission is over," the deity replied. "It's just ice cream. And cookie dough flavor, at that. You're missing out."

Whatever issue the Mother and Crone had concerning the Maiden, Sybil understood how difficult it must have been dealing with the immature deity of the waxing moon. "Very well. I shall have some ice cream."

The Maiden grinned. She brought the spoon close, and Sybil opened her mouth. The ice cream tasted good, and she finished it with a lick of her lips.

Satisfied, the moon goddess set the tub down and removed one of her earrings. A milky sphere dangled from the end of a small silver chain.

"This is a lunar stone," she said, holding the earring out to Sybil. "It will help your friend. You can craft a potion out of it, a charm, or whatever. As for contacting Selene for passage to Athens, you're a witch, you figure it out."

Sybil took the jewelry and placed it in a pocket. "Thank you, Goddess." She glanced at Cessani. "I wish to have a fair sight of Grace forthwith."

"She's in the last room down the hallway," Cessani said as she resumed typing at the computer. "Have a good time and see yourself out."

Sybil left the office and hurried down the hall. She approached the final door and found it open. Unable to pass through, she sensed a powerful blocking spell had been cast over the entrance. The invisible energy prickled her skin and rose goosebumps. The small room contained a desk, folding chair, and Grace lying on a cot.

"Sybil!" Grace exclaimed, lifting her head. "Is that really you?" Her face furrowed as she started to cry. She rose from the cot and stood just in front of the doorway.

"Don't come closer, sweet child," she said through her tears. "The barrier will knock you out." She wiped her eyes on a sleeve. "I didn't even know if you were alive, and it kept me up so many nights. Now my heart feels like it will explode from joy."

Emotion swarmed over Sybil, and she matched Grace's tears. Her heart ached, and she wanted nothing more than to throw her arms around her dear friend. Grace appeared exhausted, her blond hair disheveled and wrapped in a loosening bun. Her soiled, torn, and wrinkled clothes confirmed the reports of battling in the streets.

"My heart is so very happy to see you," Sybil managed to say. "I shall free you, Grace, I warrant."

"Don't do it, Sybil, do not go to Umaq," Grace pleaded. "Cessani told me about his plan and what she wants from you. It's too dangerous. We'll find another way."

"He must be stopped lest the world fall beneath more darkness," Sybil replied. "And I shall strive to yonder ends of the earth for your freedom. For the moment, I conceive you are safe hitherto. Knowing that fills my heart with strength."

"My dear girl," Grace said. "Please be careful. If you realize stopping Umaq is impossible, save yourself. Run far away and don't you worry about me."

Sybil raised her hand near the barrier. Grace lifted her own, their palms inches apart on either side of the doorway. They stared at each other through watery eyes, wearing small smiles.

Sybil finally lowered her arm and walked away. So much to do and think about. For the moment, she had to find Johann and somehow use the Maiden's earring to cure his illness.

Chapter Thirteen

Guilty Until Proven Innocent

Marcelo opened his eyes and found himself in a familiar place. He lay on his bed in the master bedroom of his home in Avila Beach. Yet the environment seemed false, but not dangerous. Floating above, a small moon bathed him in a comforting glow. He sat up and inspected his body. Healing burns covered his skin, the fading marks a reminder of how severe the sun damage had been. His flesh normally healed itself in a short amount of time, but the intense exposure on the mountaintop had ignited a blistering fire that nearly killed him.

He had lost consciousness sometime after Salix used her body to protect him—the dryad had saved his life. So many questions plagued him. Had his friends managed to stop both Umaq and Cessani? Salix and Johann…were they safe? If blood flowed through his dead heart, it would have pounded in anxiety over his companions' wellbeing.

As for Sybil, his true beloved, she had lain next to him some time ago. Half-conscious and unable to move on the bed, Marcelo had felt her warm body and smelled her skin. Her gentle touch and soft breath had ignited his passion to be with her. His mind had screamed at his arms to respond, for his eyelids to open, but his weakened state prevented a return caress or tender kiss on her forehead.

Although he couldn't be with her, the greatest consolation was that Sybil's visit had not been a dream. She remained safe and in good health, at least from what he sensed. However, worry closed his eyes and lowered his head. Sybil may be physically well, but what about her emotions? Something had gone amiss during the ley line travel when the group arrived during the heat of day. Marcelo only wished that guilt did not plague her. After seeing him lying in bed near death, any grief and sense of responsibility might have torn her to pieces.

"Please be well and at peace, my love," he said to the empty room.

Please be well and at peace? the demon inside Marcelo asked. *Sybil could have died in that battle because of you. You're pathetic!*

"Shut up," Marcelo told the malevolent soul. "Everyone did their best under the circumstances."

Except for you. You cowered under the dryad's body while your friends screamed in pain. You heard them. You glimpsed their agony before passing out like a weakling.

"The sun scorched my body," Marcelo retorted in anger. "There was nothing I could do."

Excuses. You could have done so much more. Submit to me, Marcelo. Become the real monster, and obtain the strength to protect your friends. Give me control and even gods will fall before you!

"I won't ever need you, demon," Marcelo said wearily.

How many centuries had he been arguing with the creature inside? How many times did he struggle to keep the monster subdued? Trying to maintain a human demeanor and the false mask of normality proved exhausting enough. The last thing he needed was endless banter by the demon soul—especially when Marcelo *did* feel weak and pathetic for not being able to help his friends.

He swung his legs off the bed and planted his feet on the floor. He tried to clear his mind and distract himself by inhaling the scent of Sybil's skin on the sheet and on his body. He then found a fresh set of clothes and dressed quickly. Glancing around for his phone, he realized it would have been destroyed by the fire. He moved toward the door and halted when someone entered.

A white gown flowed around an elderly, short-haired woman. Her withered face frowned when she saw Marcelo, azure eyes stern. "It's too soon to be out of bed," she chided. "But judging from the look on your face, nothing is going to stop you from finding Sybil."

Marcelo didn't know much about witchcraft or the goddesses of certain covens, but he recognized the presence of a deity when one stood before him. He inclined his head in respect. "Greetings, Goddess. I assume you've been taking care of me, and I am in your debt. But you're right about Sybil. Please, tell me where she and the others have gone."

"The young witch is in Salem alongside the werewolf," the deity replied. "Something about saving a friend named Grace. And the dryad is recovering in her forest home." Wearing a look of disapproval, the old goddess shook her head. "The bandages have barely hit the floor, and the four of you already wish to charge back into battle. You'll collapse from exhaustion. Or worse, get stabbed in the gut." She turned and left the room just as a second deity entered.

A goddess having the appearance of a middle-aged woman stood before him. Long white hair fell to her lower back and a matching gown covered her frame. Instead of disapproval, welcoming cobalt eyes gazed upon Marcelo.

"The Crone is not wrong, you know," she said. "All of you really should be resting now. You and your companions displayed incredible courage against Umaq and nearly lost your lives. Unfortunately, your bravery wasn't enough. The world is a different place after the sun god's death."

A weight of despair collapsed on Marcelo's shoulders. Distress filled him until it seemed his chest would burst.

"We failed to stop Umaq, then," he said softly. "Though I am relieved my friends are safe. I desire that more than anything."

"Love for those dearest to you can be a powerful motivator," the Mother replied. "Hope is not lost when you have someone to fight for. Just say the word, Marcelo, and I'll transport you to Salem."

Marcelo bowed. "Thank you for taking care of us, Goddess. It's not every day I gain an audience with a deity, and I am truly honored. I'd enjoy speaking to you more, but as you said, love and duty await. Please, send me to Salem."

The deity smiled and cast a blinding light over Marcelo. A second later, the illumination faded and he found himself in Broad Street Cemetery.

He remained still and took a moment to attune to the environment. Salem had a long history of supernatural activity. The mystical aspects seeped into every particle of soil, piece of wood, brick, or tree planted in the city. The paranormal atmosphere flooded the air, a far-reaching essence that had represented Salem's heartbeat ever since the laying of the first foundation. As part of the mystical setting, Marcelo's preternatural senses collected information through sight, sound, and smell. The sensations prickled his skin and passed over him like smoke. He detected many things, and not all of them pleasant.

Several creatures and spirits roamed the city. Old things. New things. Some only curious about the mystical imbalance, while others took advantage of the shift toward darkness. Marcelo also detected vampires, many more than he had sensed during his visit to Salem when he first met Sybil.

He stepped out of the cemetery and crossed Summer Street, then headed east on High Street. As he approached the Riley Plaza parking lot, a group of witches in red robes stopped talking and gazed at him. After a moment, one of them lit a cigarette and their conversation continued. Marcelo moved on. To those witches, he was probably just another night creature roaming the city.

However, someone did take interest when he crossed Lafayette near a Wendy's restaurant. A black Cadillac Escalade pulled up beside Marcelo. Four vampires emerged and surrounded him. He felt like Indiana Jones in the *Last Crusade* movie, when the antagonist Walter Donovan sent his cars and men to surround Indy on the street to bring him in.

"Marcelo Flores," the driver stated. "Get in the car."

Marcelo laughed. The only thing missing was the iconic Indiana Jones music to accompany the scene on the streets of Salem.

"I assure you this is no laughing matter," the driver said. "Black Jade is waiting for you."

All humor vanished as Marcelo froze. Black Jade. *Daiyu*. The ancient vampire from China had come to Salem. With over two and a half thousand years of existence, well before Christ and the Roman Empire, Daiyu's power and influence in the supernatural world resembled that of a deity. Her physical attributes made her nearly invincible. Her unlimited wisdom and experience were unmatched. With a vast network, it seemed Daiyu knew about everything and everyone. Throughout history, she had been known to either lie dormant for long periods or suddenly explode on the scene to impact critical events.

Apparently, Inti's death and the darkening of the mystical world had roused her interest. But what did she want with Marcelo? He couldn't comprehend why her attention included him in the overall situation. The questions would be answered; all he had to do was step into the vehicle.

He sat in the back between two of the vampires, and the black Escalade headed northeast on Fort Avenue. He thought Winter Island would be the destination, but the driver turned left on Memorial Drive and parked next to the small patch of sand at Dead Horse Beach.

Marcelo exited the vehicle with the others, but the vampires stayed back while he strolled across the sand by himself. Dead Horse Beach overlooked Collins Cove and Rams Horn channel. The lights of a bridge out of Salem shone in the distance, the illuminated city of

Beverly just beyond. On the darkened shore, his sharpened eyesight spotted Daiyu as she gazed out at the water.

"Thank you for coming here," she said as he approached. "I really appreciate your prompt arrival, Marcelo."

"I doubt you gave me a choice," he replied.

She looked up at him, her small frame a decoy for the immense—and terrifying—power within. "No matter. I should still be courteous and respectful."

The frigid air surrounding her didn't bother Marcelo, even as white patches of frost formed on his skin. But the enormous pressure of her aura slammed his body. He tried to remain still against the immovable force. His legs trembled and torso shook. He grunted and finally had to step back.

Daiyu pretended not to notice his discomfort as she observed the water, bare feet half buried in the sand. Her jeweled choker and matching bracelets glittered. Her dark eyes and shade of braided hair equaled the blackness of the sky.

"I've heard all about you over the centuries," Marcelo said. "I never imagined actually meeting you. Have you come to join the party in Salem?"

"You mean Cessani's moon goddess festival and monster jam? It'll keep me entertained for a while. But the real party has yet to begin. You and your friends have a maniacal demon summoner to battle. Round two."

Marcelo gazed out at the murky water. "I'm here to find Sybil. For the moment, that's all I care about."

"That's very sweet, but there are more important matters to discuss."

The air *hardened* around Marcelo—that seemed the best way to describe it. Daiyu stepped close and the destructive pressure of her aura crashed into him. His legs buckled, and he scrambled to a safe distance.

"Stay away from me," he said in irritation. "Why am I here? What do you want?"

Daiyu crossed her arms. "I recently woke from a period of dormancy to place you on trial, Marcelo Abana Flores of Spain. Former Conquistador under Francisco Pizzaro, and currently a troublesome variant that should not exist. I am your prosecutor, jury, and judge."

"What is this crazy baloney?" Marcelo scoffed. "I don't have time for this." He glanced around the beach and back to the other vampires waiting by the vehicle. Why did she bother with all the drama, secrecy, and show of force? "So you awoke to put me on an episode of Judge Judy? Or Jerry Springer? I don't even know what you're talking about."

Daiyu's grave expression remained. "I suggest you take this more seriously. Your trial began the moment you stepped on the sand, so each word you speak or action you take is marked for consideration." She stepped forward, and Marcelo retreated an equal distance. Her strict features pierced him. "Should you fail, as judge, the sentence I recommend for this matter is death."

Marcelo didn't have time for this. He longed to find Sybil, and his mind raged over the looming fight against Umaq. However, Daiyu's threat had chilled his emotions.

The sentence I recommend for this matter is death.

Marcelo's full attention bore into the ancient vampire. He did not understand this strange trial, but whatever her motivation, it would be impossible to stop her from executing the judgement. No running, hiding, or fighting could prevent his death. Daiyu could kill him on the spot if she so desired. The only way to save himself was to prove his innocence.

So let the questions begin.

"You called me a variant, one that shouldn't exist," he said. "Is that the charge?"

"It is," Daiyu confirmed. "You are a fusion of human and demon, a creature too close to identifying as a vampire and a danger to society."

Marcelo thought of the conversation he had with Johann at the bed and breakfast, about him feeling out of place. *A wannabe.* Never did he imagine that discussion would continue with his life at stake. "And what harm have I done?"

"Having an abundance of contacts and influence in the world, I completed sufficient research on you," Daiyu answered. "Why don't you ask that civilian in South Boston about harm?"

A sharp pang of remorse impaled Marcelo. The memory of tearing open a man's neck disgusted him. After battling Sybil in the streets of Boston, Marcelo had been assaulted by a gang. He could have fled the situation, but instead chose to attack and had nearly killed one of the men by consuming his blood.

No magic or coercion had propelled Marcelo. He—and the demon soul inside—desired to inflict harm...and kill. He had relished the blood in his mouth after giving in to his true nature. But blaming the demon spirit accomplished nothing. That malevolent consciousness remained a part of him, no matter how much Marcelo struggled against its reality.

"That shameful incident is something I will always regret," he said softly. "Attacking an innocent person will not happen again."

Daiyu shook her head. "So it's that easy? How can you be certain? That soul is extremely potent. Umaq is quite adept when it comes to demonic study, and he chose that specific creature for a reason. I can smell the thing inside you. I can even see flickers of its existence in your eyes. Losing control may happen again. Admit it."

Marcelo closed his eyes, his shoulders sagging from the invisible pressure of responsibility. After a moment, he gazed toward the lights of the distant bridge. "Like most vampires, I usually go to Blood Studios for a routine drink. But the demon soul yearns for violence and taking life. It…it speaks to me, and the constant fight to placate the monster is exhausting."

"You may not have said the words, but your somber tone and dejected body language will suffice as an admission," Daiyu stated.

"Acknowledging the dire possibility of losing control does not make the act inevitable," Marcelo replied. "And how am I such a danger that my existence remains on the line? Attacking a random person while suffering a moment of emotional weakness does not make me a threat to society."

"Let's say your will is strong enough to keep the demon subdued," Daiyu began. "After recent events, that means nothing since Umaq poses a danger to you. According to Cessani, he used magic to take part of the netherworld into his body. He breathes and bleeds the darkness from that realm and has become quite powerful. Having new abilities, a good chance exists that he may control you again and has stated his intention to do so. And yet, you must face him to prevent the murder of another sun god. Are you willing to expose yourself and risk falling under his command? What if he succeeds, and your fangs tear open Sybil's throat?"

"Umaq had failed after hundreds of years of preparation and would be a fool to try again," Marcelo remarked in confidence.

"I'm not willing to take that chance, which is the main reason you're on trial," Daiyu responded. "Your condition is something I will not tolerate, as you represent a black mark on my true kind. Do you know what woke me, Marcelo? It was not the sun god's demise. The shift in the natural balance, the mystical darkening, the appearance of more demons…none of that mattered to me. I would have slept right through it.

"*You* woke me. It happened in the Wyman Woods on the night Umaq cast that powerful spell to control you. Dark magic of that magnitude sent ripples throughout the supernatural world. While enchanted, you had screamed nonsense and the pissed off demon spirit hollered in rage. In the middle of it all, Umaq shouted wild commands in a crazy tug-of-war over your consciousness. The total chaos inside your head echoed across the mystical plane as your human emotions and mind shattered.

"I stirred after hearing that commotion and realized your terrifying potential for disaster. If Sybil had been turned that night, your demon essence would have passed onto her. Umaq knew what he was doing. If he had succeeded, a new race of demonic undead would have spread like disease. A cousin of the vampire and more dangerous, all under his command to wreak havoc across the planet."

"I lost control under the spell, but the incident ended without harm," Marcelo stated. "Sybil and I already proved Umaq wrong. Our love is much stronger than any dark magic he can produce."

"Don't be a naïve idiot," Daiyu snapped. "I'm offering you a fair chance to prove yourself worthy of life, however you wish to experience it. You're not human, but you enjoy acting like one. You're not a demon, yet one rages inside you. And you're registered at Blood Studios as a vampire, which you are not. You want to be in peace with Sybil? Then stop ignoring what you are, and don't pretend you're everything else."

You hear that, weakling? the demon hissed in Marcelo's mind. *You cannot ignore me forever. As much as it sickens me, we are in a symbiotic bond for survival. Accept the truth and embrace what you are. A beast! A killer!*

"I don't know what I am!" Marcelo shouted in response toward Daiyu's—and the demon's—tirade. "Whatever I'm called, I live my life as well as possible. There are good times and bad, just like for anyone else. I claim nothing and am nothing."

"Regardless, your presence has consequences," Daiyu continued. "I am prideful and protective of my vampire kin, and you are a cancer that does not belong. My problem is not with Umaq. I can prevent this disease by eliminating just one person—you."

It seemed Daiyu had already made up her mind about Marcelo's botched existence. Frustration grit his teeth, and ire clenched his fists. He had grown tired of being analyzed by those who knew nothing of his character. No warm blood stirred in his body and his heart may resemble a dead lump of ice, but raw emotions—love, remorse, and happiness—still flowed through his very being. He cherished those feelings and always realized the important things in his life. It made him human, despite what other people might categorize him as or even if he had no classification at all.

"So why don't you kill me now?" he asked in exasperation.

Daiyu smiled. "Because this is a trial. Believe it or not, I am honest and fair."

The vampire is mocking you! the demon howled. *You are entertainment for the undead, nothing more. Let me rip her face off!*

Marcelo looked away from her. He didn't doubt she could see the demon soul dancing in his gaze. "Then how do I prove my innocence and get you out of my life?"

"That's for you to figure out, Marcelo. I can't provide tips and be your judge at the same time. It would be a conflict of interest."

The heavy burden of Daiyu's threatening trial shattered Marcelo's emotions. The demon's internal coaxing scorched his nerves. The dual tension finally unraveled his patience and control.

"Then I will just kill Umaq and end it all!" he shouted.

Daiyu laughed. "Murder will make you innocent and clear your name? If you think that's the answer, then go for it. But you're too weak to face Umaq. As the world's hero, I expected more from you. Sybil disappointed me as well. She couldn't even handle a werewolf on her own. I tested her strength and left her crumpled on a rooftop. Her blood was delicious. The magic inside her tingled my tongue."

Oh my! the demon teased. *Not only did the old vampire call you weak, she hurt your lover as well.*

Marcelo didn't need a reminder from the monster. Daiyu's words burned into his mind. Her carefree tone sliced his un-beating heart. Her playful smile destroyed all reason and humanity left inside him.

Daiyu had attacked Sybil. The ancient vampire had drunk his beloved's blood. Worst of all, Marcelo really did feel weak, though not just physically. Shame and regret plagued him. The sun's flame had prevented him from helping Sybil against Umaq. Afterwards, he remained in bed while she continued to fight for him and their friends. Against Daiyu, he failed to be at Sybil's side when she needed him the most.

Love for those dearest to you can be a powerful motivator, the Mother had said. *Hope is not lost when you have someone to fight for.*

Hope? That sentiment lay buried deep in a black rage, a dark fire sweltering inside Marcelo. The beach, the water, and the other vampires disappeared in that fury. Only Daiyu existed before him…and the demon inside. In desperation, Marcelo reached into the fire and grasped onto whatever shred of hope remained before it shriveled in the blaze.

I accept the truth, he said to the demon. *Come forth, and show me who I really am!*

The demon from the nether screamed in elation. Just as Daiyu had been awakened by the commotion of Umaq's spell, she must have heard the demon's uproar again—her smile vanished in an instant.

Marcelo took a back seat to his own body, if one could describe such a thing. He released the steering wheel, let go of the shifter, and allowed the demon soul to take over as he watched the action.

He sprang forward. Blurred by intense speed, his powerful strides peppered the air in giant fans of spraying sand. Marcelo crashed against the invisible barrier surrounding Daiyu; his body slowed for an instant before shattering her aura. His arm thrust forth, and a rage-propelled fist slammed into his opponent's mouth.

Daiyu's fangs shattered. Her lips burst, and frigid, black blood sprayed her face and Marcelo's arm. Her head snapped back, and white chips of teeth sailed against the darkened sky. Her arms flailed and legs backpedaled across the sand.

However, his attack proved costly. The blow pulverized his knuckles and crushed the small bones in his right hand. The radius and ulna bones in his forearm snapped and pierced his flesh. His black, lifeless blood spewed and darkened the ground.

Marcelo stared in shock at his destroyed arm. He pushed the demon away from the steering wheel and regained control of his mind and body. Wild laughter snapped his wide-eyed gaze back to Daiyu. The ancient vampire swayed in amusement. Broken teeth fell from her open, laughter-filled mouth as replacements grew in an instant. Her lacerated lips sealed. The black blood dried in granules, and she wiped it off her pale face.

Daiyu moved so fast she seemed to teleport. She stood next to Marcelo and squeezed his shoulder in an iron grip. Her aura crushed him like a black hole and dropped him to his knees. The demon soul had retreated and remained silent; Marcelo would not be able to call upon the creature's strength. Yet even if the beast roared and taunted to come forward, Marcelo refused to become the demon's puppet again. He'd rather suffer through a Daiyu beatdown than lose himself—his real self—and give in to desperation.

"Very impressive," she said. "But that really wasn't you, was it? The subject of this trial is what managed to sock me in the face, the uncontrollable demon soul hiding within you. The jury has now experienced the true star witness, and the court is unfortunately not leaning in your favor. However, the gavel has not fallen yet. You still have time to present a case."

Marcelo trembled in effort just to move. He couldn't even raise his head to glare at Daiyu. He felt her sneer upon him. Her mocking tone added to the weight of her devastating aura. Though not painful, his right arm dangled torn and useless, a sign of failure that grounded him back to reality.

Nobody could win against Daiyu. The ancient vampire rivaled the deities from any part of the world. Marcelo could only bow in shame, his neck strained as he tried to lift his head again.

"You'll find Sybil near the witch museum," Daiyu said, releasing Marcelo's shoulder. The weight of the aura lifted as she walked away.

"Let's go back to the festival, fang gang," she called to those gathered at the vehicle.

Marcelo studied his fractured arm as the sound of an engine faded down the road. His tattered flesh started to repair, the jagged bones growing together. However, the healing process would be slow after this much damage. It seemed his shoulder had also been dislocated when Daiyu grabbed it.

He stood and cradled his arm while trudging across the sand. His injuries meant nothing when he thought of Sybil being attacked. Marcelo began to run. He had to find his beloved and somehow uncover solutions to the grave problems haunting their every stride.

Chapter Fourteen

Heart of Tears

In her home among the Klamath Mountains of southern Oregon, Salix stretched out a thin arm and observed the fresh green moss glistening on the back of her hand. Crisp leaves sprouted on her forearm. Rough, cherry-colored bark coated the outside of her elbow. Over her torso and down her legs, more leaves and patches of bark covered her green olive skin.

With the new growths on her body, the dryad had recovered from the demon attack in Machu Picchu while protecting Marcelo from not only the monsters, but the sun's harmful rays. Unlike her companion, Salix required the sun's healing light and fresh water to mend. Most importantly, the safety and comfort of her forested home provided the ideal medicine.

She picked a leaf from her arm and released it into the sweet breeze drifting through the fellow clusters of *Salix delnortensis* willow. Only audible to the dryad's sense of hearing, the leaf created a somber melody as it swirled in the wind. Each twist, turn, and flip of the leaf changed the notes in a slow rhythm and dance of sadness.

Something was wrong. Why did the leaf express grief? The breeze intensified as Salix studied the swaying movement of the surrounding treetops. A thicket rustled, and several squirrels burst forth in terror. Birds called out in alarm as they fled from branches in a spray of feathers.

A terrifying smell. Endless burning. Fire on the mountain!

Salix sprinted through foliage and past trees to head for the source. She splashed through a stream, ran up an embankment, and skidded down the other side in a small shower of dirt and stones. Panic drove her short legs and pumped the sap inside her that served as blood. She feared for the willow spirits and animals. She cried for the trees and mountain.

Ahead, thick smoke drifted over the forest and patches of fire raged across the underbrush. A massive, six-legged demon with the body of a wooly mammoth and the head of a dragon moved through the trees. It slammed against trunks and snapped them in half. Its huge, cloven feet trampled on bushes and plants.

Behind the beast, three spell casters in red robes launched fire from their hands. The hot flames ignited shrubbery and climbed up trees as black smoke curled into the air.

"Come on out here, you little forest imp!" a man shouted.

"We know you're here, dryad," a woman added. "We collected broken pieces of you at Machu Picchu and traced their origin to Klamath. Here's a little message from Umaq to anyone who interferes!" She sprayed another jet of fire toward a knot of Del Norte willow.

Having been ignited by a familiar enemy, the crackling inferno sparked another fire of rage inside Salix. She raced up a nearby tree and stood on a high branch. Wrapping her arms around the trunk, she pressed her cheek against the bark and closed her eyes to speak to the terrified wood spirit within.

Lend me your essence, dear one. Root for root, leaf by leaf, our soldiers are limitless like stars in the sky.

The bark vibrated against Salix's face, a sign of the tree's consent. Its essence pulsed within the trunk and flowed between every deep root and extended branch. The leaves stirred and danced to the wood spirit's rhythm.

Salix's right hand fused to the bark as she joined the dance. Her body swayed on the branch, head bobbing and hips rotating to the beat. In a powerful rush, the leaves tore from the branches and sailed toward the strange demon. Resembling locusts, the cloud of fast-moving leaves swarmed over the monster and sliced its flesh in hundreds of places.

The big demon roared and lurched. It suddenly bolted, strong legs thundering in a frantic escape. Caught by surprise, one of the male witches failed to move in time from the path of the creature's rabid dash. The huge beast crushed the man beneath its large hooves and rushed away, the cloud of leaves in pursuit.

Salix pulled her hand free from the trunk. She raced across a thick limb and leapt out of the knot of bare branches to sail through the air.

"I see you!" the female witch hollered.

Before Salix reached the top of an adjacent tree, a blow knocked her to the ground. The witch waved her arm. Another invisible strike blasted the dryad and sent her in a hard tumble, chunks of bark and leaves falling from her body. Salix scrambled on hands and knees to safety behind a wide trunk.

"You can't escape me, little imp!" the attacker called.

A jet of fire blasted the tree. Flames roared on either side of Salix as she hugged her knees to her chest. The intense heat blistered her green shoulders and blackened the leaves on her arms and legs. Chips of brown bark flew from her skin and turned into glowing embers.

The spray of fire subsided. Salix plunged her hands into the ground. Her fingers grew like vines, tunneling through the soil until they wrapped around the tree's roots to communicate with the injured wood spirit.

Wake, my friend. From seed to root, from stalk to branch. Stir your spirit, and free the forest of our enemy!

The ground shook. Salix heard the witch on the opposite side of the trunk shout in surprise. The dryad didn't have to witness the event to know what took place. The roots had surfaced and broke through the earth. The gnarled coils of wood wrapped around the woman's legs and held her tight.

The fire the witch generated continued to burn beneath the tree. Crackling, smoking flames slowly crept toward the woman as she struggled to escape. Her panicked attempts at magic failed to douse the blaze. Soon her struggles turned to screams—then silence—as the inferno wrapped her in its devouring embrace.

Salix rose and stepped out from behind the tree. She locked eyes with the last aggressor, his eyes wide in a pale, terrified face. He didn't even move as she walked toward him, fists clenched and purpose in her stride. Stopping before him, she gazed up at the much taller witch and pointed at the fires burning in the area.

No need for words as the man comprehended at once. He ran to the nearest patch of flames and used sprays of icy moisture from his palms to extinguish the danger. He then moved to a larger blaze consuming a clump of bushes and caused the fire to vanish. Salix followed and pointed until every lick of flame had been doused.

Sweaty and exhausted, the fear had not left the man's face as he gazed at the dryad. Salix nodded in the direction the rampaging beast had run. The witch turned and fled out of sight.

Salix looked around in grief. The fires had been extinguished, but not before the greedy element had unleashed its damage. The charred remains of bushes, blackened trees, and patches of ash resembled gray carpet.

She never imagined Umaq would focus his wrath all the way here. She had grown careless during her recovery and should have been more cognizant of her environment. As a dryad, the trees were her eyes, the wind her ears, and the *Salix delnortensis* willow her heart. Only too late had she responded to the danger. She had failed the woodland and turned her back on the mountain. But worst of all, she had harmed the Earth Mother.

Salix stomped each of her feet into the ground. Buried in the dirt, roots grew deep from her toes and heels. The roots penetrated far into the earth and plowed through dense soil and even rock. The gnarled tips moved far enough to sense the world's heartbeat, and there, Salix heard a quiet sobbing in each pulse.

Earth Mother, Salix called. *The spreading evil is greater than I imagined. As a defender of the wood, I should have been more vigilant. I am ashamed.*

No, my sweet spirit child, the Earth Mother responded. *Do not feel that way. You are a true heroine. From hemisphere to hemisphere, the wood of the world sings of your accomplishments. You bring me joy, sweet one. But you speak true of the spreading evil, and that is the foundation of my sorrow.*

I have fallen ill beneath the darkness, the Earth Mother continued. *I fear for all innocent life and the existence of this world. If another sun god's light is extinguished, the imbalance of Nature will destroy this mortal plane.*

I hear you, Mother, Salix replied. *My friends and I will restore order and eliminate the darkness. Until then, your tears are my tears. Your pain is my pain. I am sad.*

Noble creature of the leaf, the world is blessed to have you and your friends shine as stars of hope, said the Earth Mother. *The witch, the undead, and the werewolf are formidable allies. Their love for you is a shield, and your capacity to love is just as great. Nothing can break that bond.*

Salix sensed pain, grief, and anxiety roil within the Earth. The world's heart pulsed deep inside the planet. Its steady beat sent tremors throughout the continents in a series of small quakes, a warning against the perpetual darkness that may come to pass. *Thank you, dear Mother. My companions and I will ease your suffering. I am ready.*

Onward, then, said the Earth Mother. *May the tree provide shelter and the root strength. May the wind guide and the water nourish. Be well, child of the tree. The wood awaits your safe return.*

Chapter Fifteen

Howl to the Darkness

Johann's bare feet slapped the sidewalk as he sprinted down the block. Rapid breath roared in and out of his mouth. Dirt, dried blood, and scratches marred his naked body. When had he lost his clothes? He glanced behind him, then peered forward again. Had he flown in terror from something…or did he dash in pursuit of prey?

Johann had no idea why he ran in the night. No clue as to where he headed came to his distraught mind. Streetlights passed and hurled insults. The stars mocked him. Buildings hid enemies. The very street threatened to turn soft and drown him in black anguish.

He climbed over a fence and charged through grass. A park bench became a hurdle as he sailed over it. Johann splashed into a white stone fountain and finally collapsed into the shallow water.

His heartbeat boomed in his ears and temples. Hot breath burned in his lungs. A dry throat screamed for water, and he drank until a powerful cough sent him stumbling toward the edge of the fountain. Dripping, he stepped out of the water and sat glistening on a stone bench.

A mad intoxication had overtaken him. The moon goddesses had cautioned him about this, but Johann's foolish pride had ignored the threat. Worst of all, as a moment of clarity settled him, he recalled warning Sybil to run away. That seemed to be the last thing he remembered. He shuddered at the thought of having caused her harm. Where had she gone?

The transformation occurred in an instant. All lucidity vanished as the werewolf replaced the human Johann. He bolted from the seat and tore through bushes in a whirlwind of leaves and twigs. Narrow trees dotting the park snapped in half when his hairy, snarling form crashed through them. A wooden fence exploded in shards and splinters as he barreled through into the street.

He sprinted in long, bounding strides. Claws sparked on the street, and saliva streamed from the sides of his muzzle. A window-shaking howl burst from his chest. Elsewhere in the city, responding calls from his kind boomed across the sky.

He rounded a corner and a sudden, strong blow to his side knocked the werewolf into a skid across the asphalt. He recovered and observed a brown mud golem standing by the curb. Sludge dripped down its lopsided face. An elongated mouth hung beneath a pair of eyes that changed shape under each cascade of filth. The golem remained still, but Johann spotted the large dent on its muddy right foot from where it collided against his furry ribs.

Growling, Johann charged across the street and leapt at the tall creature. His claws raked through the slippery body and powerful paws sent gobs of mud flying in all directions.

A dirt-crusted fist the size of a basketball slammed into Johann's midsection. The werewolf tumbled backwards and rolled to the other side of the road. Panting, he glanced at the monster. The golem held its ground, a fresh dent on its large hand.

Johann howled in fury. With a sun god down and the barrier between worlds thinned, the amplified moonlight bathed the werewolf in powerful waves. Not even a full moon, the celestial body's sliver provided a substantial pump of strength and adrenaline.

The werewolf charged. Thick paws pounded the ground…and human hands and feet abruptly replaced them. Converted back, Johann stopped in panic and stared at the golem. The mud creature continued to stand still. Taking advantage of the large thing's odd behavior, Johann turned and jogged away.

A glance over a shoulder allowed a sigh of relief as the golem offered no indication of pursuit. A wave of nausea and dizziness sent Johann to the ground. New scrapes bloodied his knees and elbows. He held his head and wailed on the street until the debilitating sensations passed.

"Please make the pain stop," he sobbed at the twinkling sky. Another moment of clarity allowed him to think of Dom at the bed and breakfast. "Dom…I need to be with you."

Renewed madness gripped Johann and ruptured his sanity. Still in human form, he leapt up and ran down the street. A pickup truck entered an intersection and screeched to a halt in front of him. Red-robed individuals packed the bed of the vehicle.

"There's another one!" someone yelled from the passenger seat, pointing at Johann.

"Round him up!" a man hollered from the back.

Boisterous shouts erupted from the truck. Something hard and hot pelted Johann on the shoulder. He winced in pain and glanced at a blackened mark on his skin. Another blow struck his chest. The rowdy witches in the vehicle waved their arms to hurl magic projectiles. He tried to run, but a well-aimed shot spun him around. Two more strikes to his bare back forced him to move in a specific direction. The truck followed. Triumphant cries and raised fists accompanied Johann as the witches propelled him.

Blistering blows to his upper legs caused him to turn left onto another street as he jogged in agony and exhaustion. He stumbled. He stood. Blows rained on his shoulders. The truck then honked in encouragement. Witches cheered. Headlights flashed on his back in a teasing rhythm. Then the chants began.

"Wolf! Wolf! Wolf!"

The men and women in the truck lifted their voices in unison, calling for Johann to transform. He couldn't alter his form while in this deranged and uncontrollable state—at least at will—but he suspected the witches knew that. This maddening walk of shame had become entertainment for them. Earlier, a man had shouted from the truck: *There's another one!* How many other unfortunate, moon-drunk werewolves had fallen victim to this game?

Johann trudged onward. At some point he did transform, but mental and physical fatigue marred a half-hearted attempt at escape. During the chaotic effort to flee, he grew vaguely aware of having knocked a red-robed woman from the back of the truck. He also crushed in the passenger side door. Sounding as if from a distance, laughter and muffled voices accompanied his jumbled senses as he returned to human form—and the march continued.

The truck eventually parked against a curb. The witches hopped out and continued to prod Johann. The nightmare parade changed course, and cool grass replaced the hard asphalt beneath his bare feet. He tried to lay down, but a hard blow to his hip caused him to jump back up. In what appeared to be a park, a large crowd swarmed ahead amid several firepits lighting the area. Humans, undead, beasts, spirits, and other supernatural beings stood together. Cheers, gasps, and roars of excitement boomed from the throng. Where was he? What was he doing here?

"Welcome monsters, humans, and those who love to party!" an amplified voice shouted through a megaphone. "Salem Common has become your favorite battleground in the city. Bets are now being accepted for the next round of bouts. We've had some big winners tonight, so let's see that cash flow!"

Another cheer erupted from the crowd. Strong hands and magical blows shoved Johann forward. The men, women, and creatures parted to let him pass. Soon he found himself inside a wide, circular space as the horde pressed in all around.

"A new contestant has arrived!" the megaphone thundered. "Claws and snarls, fur and fangs. Get ready for another werewolf match in Salem's…,"

"Mayhem under the Moon!" the onlookers shouted in delight.

"That's right, my fellow creatures and spirits," the host continued. "Courtesy of the darkening, the moon has powered up these werewolves and made them drunk to boot. It makes a perfect combination for fights, entertainment, and money in your pocket! Now, bring out the other contestant!"

A bout of vertigo swept over Johann. Blurred faces swarmed around him. Irritating voices called and laughed. He staggered forward and tried to run through the crowd. Clawed hands, tentacles, and leathery wings shoved him back into the circle.

Using chains, a group of witches dragged a snarling gray werewolf into the makeshift arena. The wolf's claws lashed out in all directions. Its sharp teeth clicked in attempted bites at its captors. The witches unfastened the chains and pushed the wild beast toward Johann.

Hunt. Fight. Kill.

In the darkened sky, the cruel moon sang its incantation. It enraged Johann and boosted his speed, strength, and endurance. Even in human form, he did not fear the larger and stronger wolf. His hands turned into fists as he locked eyes with his nemesis.

Hunt. Fight. Kill.

Driven by moon madness, Johann charged and met the gray wolf in the center of the ring. He kicked and punched the creature. Claws and teeth slashed him in return. They wrestled, rolled, and howled amid a cacophony of spectator cheers and shouts.

Without realizing he had transformed, Johann continued to brawl in wolf form. The fight intensified. Bites, rakes, and torn fur exchanged. Why were they fighting? When did he get here?

The gray wolf shifted into a human female. Bewilderment dominated her features. She gazed at Johann as if in a trance. He sprang forward, and a hard swipe of his paw knocked her down. Sensing victory, he moved in and opened his snout, his sharp teeth over her throat.

"Please, kill me quickly," she said softly. "Make the pain stop."

Johann froze as lucidity dawned. *Make the pain stop.* He had cried those same words in the street after his fight with the golem, a moment of peace that allowed thoughts of Dom to slip through.

He gazed down at the nude female, bleeding and begging for the nightmare to end. Like Johann, the witches had dragged her here to fight for entertainment. It seemed this had been going on all night, werewolves being taken advantage of during their intoxication and torment.

Tears glistened on the woman's cheeks. Even as a wolf, Johann wept with her. He pleaded for the moon to keep him sane; a loss of control might result in the girl's death. He held her close and fought using all his heart and mind to remain in the moment. He absorbed her sadness, felt her delicate body, and thought of nothing but her.

Boos and jeers reverberated across the park. Objects pelted Johann's back. The person on the megaphone shouted. It wasn't long before the hard, magical blows peppered his body. Johann maintained his protective hold on the woman. Her trembling fingers curled into his fur. He grit his teeth against the madness. He cried, howled…and felt his mind slipping away.

A familiar set of aromas helped him remain sober: the sweet scent of lilac, fresh spun cotton candy, and a ray of bright sun after the rain. The odors wafted to him from behind the crowd. It pushed through the mix of sour sweat, dirt, and foul breath from the surrounding throng.

It seemed only a rejuvenated, three-hundred-year-old witch smelled like that.

Sybil. The young spell caster had arrived. And then suddenly, another familiar scent accompanied the witch. Cold marble, hearty wine, and old ash from a fire. Marcelo had come as well.

Releasing a final howl of joy and terror, Johann hoped he wouldn't hurt his friends as the moon illness swept over him once again.

Chapter Sixteen

Unstoppable

In the dim light of his chambers in the stone hovel, Umaq dressed in haste. So much work remained before his departure to Greece, and he had wasted enough time already. Through the window, the sun began to set over Machu Picchu and the sky blazed a fiery orange.

A cold, strong hand clamped around his wrist. "What's the rush, stupid human?" a husky voice called from the bed.

Umaq jerked his arm free and slipped a shirt over his torso. He then stared at the naked demon, Zelaenah, lying on the mattress. Her charcoal-colored skin glowed in the setting sun's light bathing her through the window. Her bald head sat propped on an arm; two more arms lay at rest, and the fourth draped across her leg after he had shaken off her grip. The demon's six breasts hung exposed, her bird feet curled by the crumpled sheet. Fierce gold eyes contained a hint of mockery as she returned an intense stare.

Zelaenah's stench no longer bothered Umaq. Over the last several days, he had somehow grown acclimated to the demon's smell. One moment it was there, the next gone. He collected his pants from the floor and stepped into them.

"The rush is me trying to attain my lifelong goal," he said. "Killing Inti was part of it. But unifying the demon kingdom with this realm is my ultimate ambition."

"You didn't seem so worried about time a few moments ago," Zelaenah replied. "To think I allowed a human to sleep with me. How low I have fallen."

"You didn't allow anything," Umaq answered. "I take what I want."

"Is that so?" Zelaenah asked. "Are you enjoying your new dark power, the one you siphoned through that window connected to my world?"

"Yes, I'm relishing it," Umaq said, tying his shoes. "I told you. I take what I want."

Zelaenah slid off the mattress and stood, then crossed all four arms. "And pissed off the underworld gods while doing so. Using black nether energy to defeat Inti is one thing, but taking it into your body for personal gain while claiming equivalence to the deities? That's another level of stupid entirely. Do you believe your egotism will go unpunished? I can't wait to see the dark gods rip your flesh off."

"You should know by now I think very little of any deity," Umaq retorted. "Gods do not control my destiny. They have proven their ineptness over the ages, and the underworld ones are no different. They should be thanking me for tearing down the gate between our worlds."

Zelaenah's golden eyes widened in surprise. "Like I said, I can't wait to see you punished." She then smiled, a grotesque expression of sharp teeth and cruel intent. "And I'll be the one holding you down while you scream."

Umaq stared at the higher tier demon, a strong and intelligent monster standing above the mindless worker horde in Machu Picchu. She may be under his control, but he couldn't prevent the beast from speaking her mind. In that moment, Zelaenah represented the dark gods and acted as their spokesperson. The creature embodied everything Umaq hated.

Shouting in rage, he drove a hard fist into the demon's face, and her head snapped backward. She stumbled and fell onto the bed, laughing in a wild fit.

"Be thankful I don't kill you," he uttered over the clamor.

"Now, you really shouldn't alienate yourself," Zelaenah replied after her mirth subsided. "You have no friends, only enslaved demons who despise you." The dark creature leaned forward and spat on the floor.

Umaq grabbed the ley staff from a table and ran a finger along the light blue shaft. World Key, he had named it, a tuning fork to travel the planet and unlock his destiny of conquest. "I could care less about your kind. You are nothing but tools and a means to an end."

"That's how you treated Cessani and look what happened," Zelaenah observed. "The death of Inti has strengthened those witches, and now her followers are growing. She is sponsored by moon deities and plays queen in Salem. Cessani has no more use for you. In fact, reports from Salem indicate she had a chance to capture Sybil, but instead sided with the young witch to try and stop you from destroying Helios. She betrayed you."

Umaq picked up a blue, oval shaped ring also crafted from ley stone and slipped it over his fingers like a set of brass knuckles. This instrument worked in unison with World Key. During his experiments to access a ley gate, he discovered striking a piece of ley stone against the tuning fork proved necessary to create the right frequency to split the earth. Like a music composer's baton, the oval ring served as a method to enlarge and enhance the sweet melody humming from the staff.

"Cessani will need me more than ever after I succeed in Athens," said Umaq. "Her influence among witches is not as solid as she believes. Without her knowing, I sent a few of her coven members and a demon to eliminate the dryad. As for Sybil and her other infuriating friends, I welcome the opportunity to face them again. For over three hundred years that little witch has been an obstruction to my achievements. No moon goddesses or miracles will save her this time."

"At least you and I now agree on something," Zelaenah admitted. "The joy of inflicting violence on those pests will serve as compensation for having to suffer through your…" She glanced down at his crotch. "Desires," she finished in a scowl.

The ley staff and oval ring in hand, Umaq turned and headed for the door. "Don't fool yourself, demon. It wasn't exactly pleasurable." Zelaenah's shrill laughter followed him as he headed outside.

Umaq crossed the residential district as the sun lowered on the horizon, the fading light of dusk blanketing Machu Picchu. He left the stone walkways and strode onto the soft grass of the Central Plaza.

Here, a black tide of demonic terror awaited him. Nearly a thousand creatures from the netherworld packed the field. Horrid beasts roared in spine-chilling bursts. Others paced in restless circles, their sharp claws puncturing the field. However, the more frightening demons did nothing. They stood in quiet contemplation with expressive eyes, their patience a gift and intellect a weapon.

The dark mass parted to let Umaq through as he performed an inspection like a general examining his troops. Sets of different colored eyes watched him pass. Nostrils flared as the creatures sniffed. Demons of all size shifted their weight in anxiety. Throats growled, hooves pawed the ground, and wings flapped. Barks, howls, and murmured conversation moved through the horde.

Satisfied, Umaq left the grass area to enter the stonework of the Sacred Plaza. He strolled past the Temple of the Three Windows and ascended the steps toward the altar of Intihuatana. Behind him, the demons followed in a long train of malice and desire to cause havoc in this world. He sensed their impatience to destroy the barrier between planes and unite the underworld with this realm. The creatures longed for a new territory to invade and inflict suffering upon.

However, explosive hatred for him is what Umaq felt spewing from the demons the most. He had enslaved them, after all—a dupe after opening the portal to invite them in. Like Zelaenah, these creatures desired nothing more than to eat him alive after having been tricked into submission.

Umaq reached the top of the hill and entered the small courtyard. The charred altar where he had struck down Inti sat a short distance away. On the opposite side, the ruined temple where he had performed the ley gate experiments stood shadowed in the dying light.

He moved through the crumbled wall and entered the chamber where Sybil and her friends had blasted through using the ruptured ley line. The mystical energy remained strong here and provided the best place in Machu Picchu to open a gate.

The demon throng milled in the courtyard and crowded the stairs as Umaq held up World Key. In the last of the day's light, he struck the forks of the ley staff using the oval ring on his opposite fist.

A melodic hum burst from the staff. Its rich tone filled the ruined chamber and reverberated off what remained of the stone walls. The ground shook. Cracks raced along the flagstone floor, and a large gap opened in the ancient temple. Vivid blue light erupted from the hole. Umaq stepped back as a wave of mystical energy swept through the chamber. The demons called out in their language, snorted, and gnashed their teeth in restless anticipation.

"Into the pit, my underworld guests!" Umaq shouted. "The bowels of the earth await us. We will journey past desert, forest, mountain, and ocean toward victory. Helios the sun god will fall, boundaries will shatter, and this world will be ours to command!"

The dark mass of beasts piled into the chamber and leapt into the breach. Umaq halted the train when the tuning fork's hum reached its end and the floor closed. He struck World Key again and the fissure yawned open to the sound of a shrill, wavering note that rose goosebumps on his skin. The ley staff had to sing four more times before the last of the demons poured through.

A clammy hand gently closed around Umaq's neck. Accustomed to Zelaenah's smell, his nose failed to detect her, but her touch over the past several days had grown familiar. However, the caress on his throat lacked any affection. He smiled as the female demon stood behind. She trembled in effort to choke him to death, but unable due to his power of control.

He turned and met her striking gold eyes. "Are you ready to fight another sun god?"

Out of breath, Zelaenah released her weak grip and stood back. "I am," she replied in a harsh tone. "Are you certain you know how to transport us in that pit?"

Black, smoky tendrils of nether energy coiled from Umaq's body and into the air. He closed his eyes and savored the thrill of his newfound power. "I am absolutely certain."

World Key sang for the final time that day as total darkness now covered the mountain citadel. A gap split the chamber floor, and Umaq dropped into the shining blue light with Zelaenah at his side.

Chapter Seventeen

Remedy for the Rabid

Sybil exited the former witch museum and waded into the throng of supernatural entities mingling outside. Floating ethereal spirits chased each other through the crowd. Chatty fairies played dice games on the sidewalk. A group of sirens, pale and elegant, sang around the dancing flames of a fire pit. Centaurs drank and laughed with witches. Small, winged demons sailed overhead.

A knot of vampires conversed near the street, and eye contact with Daiyu froze Sybil. The ancient Chinese undead smiled and shrugged her narrow shoulders as if to ask, *What are you going to do about it?* Black Jade's assault on the rooftop, the threat to Marcelo, and her enjoyment of the growing darkness boiled Sybil's blood.

Somehow, she managed to subdue her explosion of anger. This was not the time or place to fight such a powerful foe. Sybil needed to leave this nest of hornets and find Johann. The poor werewolf suffered under the moon's amplification and mystical imbalance. The Maiden's earring provided a solution to ending his torment. She had to hurry before her friend harmed himself or an innocent person.

Leaving the monster revelry, she headed south on Washington Square, but didn't get very far before a roar of voices caught her attention. She faced the source of the big uproar somewhere in the field of Salem Commons. Sybil stepped through a line of trees that bordered the grassy park and gaped at another raucous gathering near the white gazebo.

Creatures and humans formed a large ring of cheers, boos, and flailing arms as they clapped or threw objects. Above all the clamor, the distinct sound of werewolves snarling, howling, and crying in pain shocked her. Fearing it could be Johann, she strode through the crowd in panic and elbowed her way toward a clearing in the center of the mob.

Sybil burst into the ring and gasped in horror. She recognized Johann's werewolf form, his shaggy blond fur matted by dirt and blood. Tufts of hair littered the torn grass. Pinned beneath him, a battered naked female lay half-conscious.

"Johann!" Sybil screamed.

The poor werewolf met her eyes, his dazed expression filled with pain and confusion. Saliva oozed from his muzzle. The moon intoxication held him tight in its cruel grasp. And these boisterous, callous humans and monsters reveled in amusement from her dear friend's agony.

It reminded Sybil of Daiyu. *Your entertainment hath been birthed from my misery!* she had told the heartless vampire.

Sybil took a deep breath and screamed in fury. Her amplified voice traveled in a shimmering wave and knocked scores of humans and creatures to the ground. Johann howled and bolted past the fallen onlookers. She sprinted after him, then halted when a familiar voice called her name. She turned and saw Marcelo climbing to his feet. Apparently, her mega shout had bowled him over as well.

"Marcelo!" she cried.

"I'm so glad to see you!" he exclaimed. "I've been looking for you and just arrived. What's going on here, are you all right?"

She threw herself into his arms and melted against his body. The embrace filled her with burning love that warmed her head to toe. She breathed in his scent and closed her eyes, the chaos in the aftermath of her scream forgotten.

After a moment of quiet bliss, Sybil glanced at the crowd. Not too concerned with the end of the wolf brawl, most of the audience had broken off into smaller groups to chat by the firepits. Others attempted to reform the fighting ring, but had no success. Several beasts and humans threw her hate-filled glances and muttered curses.

Sybil then realized Marcelo only held her using one arm. She pulled back and stared in shock at his misshapen, fractured right hand and forearm. Before she could speak, he swept her into a long, passionate kiss.

She retreated again, breathless, but wouldn't be distracted by his affection. "Marcelo, your arm!" she observed in total distress. "It hath been completely destroyed." She reached out to treat the gruesome injury with a spell, but he moved his arm away.

"The injury will heal on its own, love," he said calmly. "It actually looks a lot better than before." He tried to move his fingers, but only the thumb and forefinger wiggled. "There are twenty-seven bones in the hand, and I think eight of them are restored." He grinned.

Sybil did not smile. She knew Marcelo rarely felt pain, and even if the damage didn't bother him, this was no laughing matter. His arm had suffered a severe trauma. Not many beings—supernatural or human—could harm him in that manner. And hadn't he been resting with the Mother and Crone not too long ago?

"Your arm…tell me wherefore," she demanded, trying to hide the apprehension in her voice.

Marcelo glanced at her left arm. "First, tell me about your burnt wrist."

Sybil's cheeks heated as she moved her hand behind her back. She had nearly forgotten her own wound while worried for Marcelo. Daiyu's grip had seared Sybil's skin and magic only produced slight healing. She couldn't exactly chastise him about his injury while having one of her own.

She finally glanced in the direction Johann had run. "Johann does not fare well, the moon hath made him ill. It behooves us to catch him forthwith, so we ought to discuss this later."

Marcelo nodded, an intense concern in his eyes that matched her own. "At least my legs are working fine. Let's hurry."

Side by side, they jogged away from the crowd to find Johann. Sybil clenched her fists as she ran. Marcelo had avoided the question about his injury, but she suspected the answer and it made her even more terrified. No one else in the immediate area desired to hurt Marcelo except Daiyu. The powerful vampire had already threatened him and hurt Sybil. Had Black Jade already attacked him?

"Any idea how to help Johann?" Marcelo asked as they left the park. "If we manage to tie him up or corner him, then what? And what about Grace? The Mother said she may be in trouble, and I can't stop worrying."

South of Salem Common, Sybil stopped on the corner of Essex and Union Street. She told him about her encounter with Cessani and the Maiden.

Marcelo closed his eyes, the suppressed anger filling his features. "At least we know where Grace is. She will be safe for the time being, as bizarre as that sounds."

"You speak true," Sybil agreed, recalling her odd meeting inside the former witch museum. "As for Johann, I am conversant on a solution using yonder moon goddess's earring. However, I shall require a sundry of ingredients for spell casting."

"Now that I can help with, but I'll need to borrow your phone," he said. Sybil handed it over, and he tapped the screen a few times. "I found a witchcraft store near the water south of here, hopefully away from most of the monster activity. With the city in chaos, we're not going to find an Uber or taxi anywhere. And my poor car…" He trailed off and sighed while returning the phone. "My poor car is still parked in Oregon near Crater Lake. We'll have to get our cardio in with some more jogging. Follow me."

Sybil just realized they had been standing next to the Bella Verona restaurant. A touch of nostalgia—and humor—filled her when she glanced inside the window as she passed. It seemed years had gone by since she stumbled out of the Salem Witch Museum as an old woman after sleeping for over three centuries—lost, confused, and frightened of this time period. She had devoured the food off someone else's plate, knocked the manager out using a sleep spell, and fled.

Marcelo had later found her by the lighthouse, alone and angry with her box of takeout. Madness surrounded her in this new world, but Marcelo had been the one thing that kept her grounded in reality and free from insanity and despair. Even now, with the entire world turned upside down, he continued to be her anchor of support in thought, word, and emotion. She loved Marcelo—the human, the undefined vampire, and even the malevolent demon. Those categories signified his greatest strengths and weaknesses. But together, all three represented a greater whole, one that cared for Sybil and showed her tremendous love.

From the corner of her eye, she watched him jog at her side. He moved with the purpose of protection and an endless sense of justice to help his friends and loved ones. One arm swung in its awkward break after each stride. But even when vulnerable, an indescribable strength radiated around Marcelo, a sensation that motivated Sybil and brought forth a strength of her own.

They continued south on Union Street until it turned into Wharf Street. As the road swept around some buildings and started to curve back toward the north, Marcelo trotted off between two of the structures. Sybil observed a sign for a store called Antiques Gallery, and right behind it was a witchcraft shop called The Cauldron Black. Marcelo neared the darkened entrance and glanced around, but Sybil hadn't seen anyone at all. With monsters running through the streets and witches on patrol, she assumed most of the anxious citizens had locked themselves in their homes.

Marcelo kicked the door open in a loud crash. "Ready for business," he said, bowing.

Due to the urgency of the situation, Sybil didn't have time to feel guilty for not only breaking and entering, but also stealing. Using her phone as a flashlight, she quickly searched inside for a few things necessary for the spell: cinnamon oil, rosemary oil, a clove of garlic, a black candle, and a small ritual knife with healing runes etched on the blade.

"So how will the spell work?" Marcelo asked as he stood guard by the entrance. "I hope we don't need to sacrifice any cows."

Sybil clucked her tongue. "I think not, silly. I shall make a potion for Johann to drink and a special oil to eliminate negative energy in his disquieted mind."

She placed the spell items on the checkout counter, then studied a glass jar full of souvenir pencils having witch hats for erasers. She shook out the pencils and placed the Maiden's earring next to the empty jar.

"Can I help with anything?" Marcelo asked.

"I shall require something heavy to smash the earring," Sybil answered, glancing around the shop. "Yonder moon stone must be turned into powder, lest the potion shall not work."

"Pass me the earring," Marcelo said, walking over. "I want to try something."

She placed the jewelry in his undamaged left hand. He wrapped a fist around the moon stone, and grunting, squeezed the earring hard enough to make his entire arm shake. After a moment, he uncurled his fingers and revealed a small pile of moon dust.

"Hah!" he exclaimed. "Look at that strength. Just like Superman."

"Superman?"

"Never mind," he said with a grin. "I'll just make note of another set of movies we need to watch."

"Truly, I look forward to having a fair sight of them," Sybil replied, her interest keen. "You are conversant on how much my heart is pleased with *moovys*." She held out the glass jar. "Place the powder inside forthwith."

Marcelo carefully dumped the moon powder into the container.

Sybil smiled. "The potion is ready, I warrant. Only water remaineth."

Marcelo laughed. "That's it? Look at me doing magic." He nodded toward the other items on the counter. "What about all that?"

"The potion seems simple, but of a truth, the additional spell shall require more preparation." She looked toward the door in growing apprehension. "Little time remaineth. I require a quiet and safe place to perform the enchantment. Chasing Johann around yonder city ought to be difficult enough, and we shall also strive to seek an adequate location afterwards."

"Why don't you stay here, and I'll go after Johann," Marcelo suggested. "That will give you time to set up, and this place seems safe enough. I'll bring him back, no worries."

But of course she worried. His arm appeared to have healed more, but Johann proved to be out of control. She had barely escaped harm the first time and thought both of them would be required to subdue the rabid werewolf.

Marcelo seemed to read the concern in her gaze; he moved in and kissed her before she could protest. He pulled back and caressed her cheek.

"I love you," he said softly. "I'll return as soon as I can."

"I love you, too," she replied, then watched for a moment as he headed out the door.

Sybil went to work and tried to concentrate without thoughts of Marcelo alone in the crazed streets of Salem. Sweating, she pushed aside some shelves to clear space on the floor. She moved smaller displays aside and collected several colored candles to set out in a wide circle. The pink candle inspired a calming sense of peace and balance. Yellow, sunny and joyful, improved mood and offset stress. The blue candle also represented a color of peace, to inspire a powerful sense of calm.

With the ring of candles complete, she began to produce the banishing oil. From the counter, she took the cinnamon and rosemary oils and mixed them in a glass vial. The cinnamon oil not only boosted the function of herbs and plants, but it especially provided protection from negative energy. The rosemary oil also dispelled negative forces while offering protective and transformative properties.

Sybil used the ritual knife to cut the garlic clove into several small pieces, then added them to the oil inside the vial. Combined with the two oils, the garlic added strong defensive energies while also expelling malevolent qualities.

She placed the completed banishing oil on the counter and picked up the jar with the crushed moon powder inside. Walking around the shop, she searched for a source of water to mix with the powder. Sybil stepped between the shelves, checked the storeroom in the back, and examined behind the counter. Nothing. The small shop also lacked a working sink. Growing desperate, she even looked inside the garbage can for a half-filled bottle of water or soda—anything!

"Truly, I refuseth to believe nothing is present to drink hither," she stated to the empty shop.

Sybil felt ridiculous. She had taken the most common and abundant resource for granted. She didn't even think about water until the last moment. Johann couldn't drink the potion without an edible liquid.

Pacing, she dug her phone out of a pocket and searched for a grocery store, gas station, restaurant, or any place she could get a beverage from. Smiling in relief, she found the Sea Level Oyster Bar about a hundred feet away, right across the road.

Tall lampposts illuminated the area as Sybil walked outside and crossed Wharf Street. Directly in front of the restaurant, a narrow strip of water contained several white boats bobbing next to a string of docks. The canal eventually met with Salem Harbor before opening out toward the Atlantic. Seawater wouldn't do for the potion. Salt would tarnish the properties of the moon powder, and she doubted anyone could even keep ocean water down.

She approached the glass door to the Sea Level Oyster Bar. Extending an arm, she shattered the glass panes using a hard blast of air and carefully moved inside.

"I am sorry," she said in genuine guilt.

Sybil stepped over the broken glass and past several tables with overturned chairs set on top. After locating the kitchen, it didn't take long to find a small can of pineapple juice, one more likely to be used in preparing mixed beverages at the bar. Carrying the prize, she turned to leave, but halted when seeing a basket of lemons on the counter.

Lemon rind could be used in the banishing oil as another key ingredient to cleanse negative energy and remove the blockages in one's path. Along with the cinnamon, rosemary, and garlic, the added lemon would provide a much more effective result.

Sybil quickly opened cabinets and drawers to search for a cheese grater. Finding one, she set it on the counter and scraped a lemon several times to produce a small pile of grated rind. She scooped the granules onto a napkin and folded it several times to place in a pocket. She grabbed the pineapple juice on the way out of the kitchen, then halted near the front of the restaurant.

A man wearing pajama pants and a t-shirt stood holding a rifle pointed at Sybil's chest. His dark hair looked mussed as if he had just woken.

"What the hell are you doing in my restaurant?" he asked in a gruff voice.

Sybil's heart pounded. "I…I mean no harm, truly. I just—"

"Damn looters," the man interrupted. "You lot will take advantage of any bad situation. Cessani and her witch revolution is destroying Salem. The mayor and some police have already accepted defeat. The cops may not respond to the restaurant's silent alarm, but I sure as hell will." He nodded toward the juice can. "What else have you taken? Empty your pockets or I'll empty your skull."

"Please," Sybil said softly, fighting panic.

She still had to finish setting up for Johann. How soon would Marcelo return…was he all right? How could she convince this livid man to lower his weapon and go away? "I only wish to aid a friend with a spell…"

The man's eyes widened. Sybil then realized her mistake—her rattled nerves caused her to admit the wrong thing.

"A spell…you're one of Cessani's witches!" he shouted. "My neighbors and I are locked in our homes, terrified to come out with wild monsters in the streets. Our city is a prison. You witches may take our freedom, but not my family's livelihood. This restaurant is everything to me!"

Despite the dangerous situation, Sybil's heart went out to him. Beneath the raw anger and behind the steel of his rifle, fear and desperation motivated this citizen of Salem. In this moment, Sybil represented Cessani and all the red-robed witches controlling the city. She characterized the beasts, demons, and feral spirits roaming the chaotic streets. The man's life—and thousands of other lives and loved ones—had been upended in darkness. The common citizens couldn't fight against Cessani and her supernatural machine. But in this tiny corner of Salem, protecting a restaurant and means to support a family solidified the man's courage to make a stand.

Unfortunately, Sybil had her own motivations to fight. She needed to end this situation in haste.

Outside, an approaching motor roared into the canal. The man glanced through the window. Sybil took advantage of the distraction and launched a spinning knot of air toward him. The fist-sized blast slammed into his body. He tumbled into a table and stack of chairs. The rifle slipped from his grip and skidded across the floor.

Sybil ran to the weapon and picked it up, then bolted outside through the broken door. She glanced toward the canal and spotted the source of the engine noise—Marcelo steering a small boat next to one of the short docks. After stationing the vessel and cutting off the motor, he reached toward a seat and lifted an unconscious Johann, in human form, over his shoulder.

"Marcelo!" she called from the street. "Make haste, come inside yonder magic shop."

Marcelo climbed out of the boat and stepped onto the dock. Being careful with Johann, he hurried to meet Sybil and they headed inside The Cauldron Black.

"What in the world are you doing with that rifle?" he asked in alarm while laying the werewolf on the floor. "Sheesh, I can't ever leave you alone for a minute."

Sybil set the rifle aside and knelt next to Johann. He wore a hoodie and sweatpants, his hands and feet bound by rope. She caressed the poor man's forehead and observed his slow breath, his pale features marred by scratches, dirt, and exhaustion.

She sighed and explained her encounter at the restaurant. "I did not wish to harm yonder citizen, I warrant."

"You did what was necessary, and I'm glad you're all right," Marcelo said. "What should I do to help with the spell?"

"Place Johann in the center of the candles and light them using yonder matches on the floor. I shall prepare the potion and banishing oil." Sybil opened the can of pineapple juice and poured the drink into the jar with the moon dust. She noticed Marcelo's hand and arm appeared much better than before. "Truly, you sought Johann having great success and must have striven with all your heart." She smiled at him. "Curiosity overcomes me at how you became a pirate captain on yonder boat."

Marcelo smiled as he slid Johann into place and collected the matchbox, then lit the candles. "I followed the wild howls, his scent, and the trail of debris as he rampaged south of here. I finally found him asleep and naked in the baseball field by Palmer's Cove. He must have been totally exhausted. As for becoming a pirate, I broke into the Palmer's Cove Yacht Club to steal keys to a boat. I also found some clothes for Johann in a gym bag. I felt bad tying him up, but I couldn't take any chances."

"They're inside The Cauldron Black!" a familiar voice yelled from outside. "A witch stole my rifle, and I saw an undead carry a body inside the store. They broke into my restaurant, and now they're looting the magic shop."

It seemed the man had witnessed some of the activity from the oyster bar, then called someone for assistance. He had spoken true about the police not being around, so had more civilians come to the man's aid?

"We all need to fight for our neighborhood," another voice responded, followed by a chorus of approvals. "These are our stores and restaurants. We need to defend what little freedom we have left in Salem. Cessani and her horde will not have their way!"

The window shattered as a bullet zipped into the store. Sybil nearly dropped the potion as she ducked. Marcelo grabbed a shelf and dragged it to the window for protection. Another bullet tore through the door. She helped Marcelo push another shelf and a cabinet against the entryway.

"Finish the preparation," Marcelo said, his body tense and eyes on the barricade. "They won't get inside. I'll make sure of it."

"Be careful," she told him.

Hands trembling, Sybil removed the folded napkin from her pocket and dumped the grated lemon rind into the vial containing the cinnamon and rosemary oils. The banishing concoction should be left for a night to allow the ingredients to settle and increase potency, but she only had a few minutes as another round of bullets peppered the barricade.

She stepped into the circle of colored candles and applied dabs of the banishing oil across Johann's forehead, on the backs of his hands, and just above his ankles. She froze when he stirred. He opened his eyes and looked at her in a daze, then suddenly shouted and began to struggle.

"Marcelo!" Sybil called. "He hath awoken. We must give him the potion forthwith."

"Get it ready," Marcelo answered. "But first, cover your ears." He grabbed the rifle and fired three loud shots through the window, aimed well over the attackers' heads. "That should back them off for a minute. Let's do this!"

He joined Sybil in the circle. Marcelo threw himself on top of Johann, then wrapped his arms and legs around the struggling man. "I hope he doesn't transform. I don't think I'd be able to hold him."

Sybil added to the pile when she sat on both men. Holding the pineapple and moon dust potion in one hand, she gripped Johann's chin with the other and slowly poured some of the liquid into his mouth. Marcelo squeezed the werewolf using one arm while the other clamped a hand over Johann's mouth.

The distraught man coughed against Marcelo's palm, but Sybil watched his throat as he swallowed in reflex. In coordination with Marcelo, she repeated the process two more times until Johann consumed the last of the potion.

Sybil hovered a palm over the werewolf's face. What resembled black snowflakes fluttered from her hand and settled over his eyes, nose, and mouth. After another round of struggles, his movements lessened, and he fell into a deep sleep.

"Forthwith the final part hath arrived," said Sybil. She hurried to the black candle on the counter and used the ritual knife to carve the following words on the dark wax: Moon Rage, Stress, Suffering. She lit the candle and nodded at Marcelo. "All that remaineth is to wait till yonder candle burns out."

"You never cease to amaze me," he remarked. "You truly are incredible, Sybil."

"I am on occasion, I warrant," she replied, winking.

A bullet slammed into the blocked door. "Give yourselves up!" someone shouted from outside.

"We can take care of the other problem out front now," said Marcelo. "Besides waiting for the black candle to burn, our work is done here, right?"

Johann moaned. He rolled over in his restraints, twitched, then remained still.

Sybil shook her head. "My heart fears to leave him be. Johann's disquieted mind is strong, thus he may wake again. He ought to remaineth inside the circle of candles."

Marcelo moved Johann back to where he was before the roll, directly in the center. "Then we'll hunker down until the candle is gone. Hopefully the cowboys outside will get bored and leave."

Time passed as they waited. An occasional gunshot exploded against the barrier and sent wood splinters flying. The men shouted insults or taunts. Every now and then, Marcelo returned a shot from the rifle to keep the attackers from getting close.

Finally, the black candle reached its end. The flame sputtered and died in a pool of hot wax. Some of the colored candles in the circle had already snuffed themselves out. Sybil crawled across the floor and knelt over Johann while Marcelo watched the entrance. She snapped her fingers near the werewolf's ear, and his eyes opened.

"Sybil?" Johann asked. He sat up and glanced around the ruined shop, then flinched as a bullet blasted the wall. "This place is a wreck, you and Marcelo are here, and danger is right outside. Why am I not surprised to find myself in this situation?"

Relieved, Sybil hugged him tight, then worked to remove the cords from his wrists and ankles. "'Tis good to see you well. You are no longer ailed by yonder moon's imbalance. However, a sundry of angry citizens believe we are the enemy and have come hither."

Free from the restraints, Johann threw his arms around Sybil and kissed her cheek. "I owe the both of you my life. I only recall scraps of memory, but what I can remember is not pleasant. I hope I haven't harmed anyone…or worse."

"Well, you mostly harmed yourself," Marcelo commented as he came over and embraced his friend. "Johann, now that you've returned to your senses, do you still wish to continue with us to stop Umaq? I understand if you'd rather be with Dom. I'll get you home safely, I promise."

Tears welled in Johann's eyes. "Thank you, Marcelo. I miss Dom, but I'm seeing this through until the end. After all, we have a world to save." He glanced around again. "All we need is Salix. Where is my little plant face?"

"Truly, I do not know if she is ready to be summoned hither," Sybil replied. She removed the short twig from her back pocket. "The Crone said this may be used to call the dryad, but I wonder if she hath been healed yet."

The stick suddenly grew warm in Sybil's hand. A single leaf sprouted from one end. The small branch vibrated. Another leaf budded in the middle.

"Something is happening," she said in wonder. She placed the wood on the floor, and they gathered around.

The twig elongated and thickened. It rolled back and forth across the tile. Crisp leaves burst to life. New branches grew and snaked in all directions. Moss appeared in vibrant patches. Soon flesh took form, the color of a green olive and coated in random patches of cherry bark. A body and head became discernable. Arms and legs writhed into life. Vivid emerald eyes, filled by the light of the world, fashioned on a beautiful face having a tiny nose and no mouth.

Salix stood before them, unable to smile, but radiating such joy that it penetrated Sybil's heart and soothed her mind. She could tell the others felt the same emotions from the dryad. Marcelo grinned and Johann cheered. Sybil wiped her happy tears, and everyone closed in to throw their arms around Salix.

"I missed you so much, dear dryad," Sybil whispered. "My heart hath been relieved to see you."

I missed you as well, Spell Weaver. Salix brushed a finger across a patch of moss to speak. *Marcelo's, Johann's, and your thoughts of me were sufficient to call me forth. We have work to do. I am ready.*

A bullet tore a chunk from the door and slammed into a shelf. In anger, Johann threw off his stolen garments. He transformed in an instant; his furry werewolf shape stood huge inside the small shop. A deep, powerful howl burst from his chest. Sybil covered her ears as the piercing cry seemed to shake the walls and ceiling.

The howl ended, and the men outside shouted in alarm. "There's another monster in there!" someone yelled. "Move back!"

Johann reverted to human form and donned his clothes and shoes. "Forgive the sudden nudity. I usually have several beers before something like that happens."

Marcelo laughed, then fired an additional round through the window for added menace. "Sorry, Salix. Bad timing on your arrival. We're in a bit of a squeeze here." He looked at Sybil. "Now can we end this?"

Sybil smiled. "I have a better idea, I warrant. Cessani hath explained that Helios, the sun god, is Umaq's next target in Athens. I must contact his sister, the Moon Goddess Selene. Of a truth, the lunar deity shall take us after I summon her hither. It shall not be necessary to strive against yonder citizens out front."

Johann let out a low whistle. "Call a moon goddess? I imagine that would take quite a bit of magic, and time."

"It shall not require any magic and only a few moments, truly," Sybil replied. She looked at each of her beloved friends. "All I need is prayer."

Chapter Eighteen

When Gods Tremble

"Umaq and his demons have arrived in Athens," said Helios, the Greek sun god.

He stood from the white marble bench and paced the tiled floor of the temple. His white linen chiton, a type of tunic, draped from one shoulder. Belted at the waist, the flowing fabric hung to his ankles and swished around his sandaled feet as he moved.

Selene, Goddess of the Moon, watched her brother with sympathy…and growing fear. "I know, dear brother, I can feel their dark presence." She strolled to his side, her long peplos gown made from folded fabric brushing the floor. "I will fight by your side to drive this menace from our world."

"You have my gratitude, dearest sister. But honestly, will just the two of us be enough?" Helios wouldn't stop pacing as anxiety dominated his features. "Inti was a mighty sun god and a fierce warrior. In the end, he couldn't stand against Umaq and his powerful allies. The Inca demon master is simply too strong."

Selene looked up at the tall marble columns surrounding them in the temple foyer. Vines hung between the columns like curtains, and various potted plants decorated the area. In the distance, the sound of a large water fountain usually soothed her, but today the gentle cascades brought no comfort.

Who do gods pray to at a time like this?

"Brother, we can—"

A sudden whisper halted Selene's words. She glanced around, but saw nothing. "Did you hear that?"

Helios finally stopped pacing as he regarded her in wonder. "No, I didn't hear anything. What are you referring to?"

Selene's skin tingled. Her heart now fluttered and warmth filled her cheeks, odd sensations she hadn't experienced in years when…could it really be?

"Helios, someone is praying to me!" she said in surprise. "How ironic. A person is calling to me in the very moment I'm thinking about who to contact for aid." She moved away a few steps. "I can barely hear them. Give me a moment."

The ancient days of Greece had long passed. Many Greek deities had grown irrelevant, forgotten over the centuries as religions changed or the fickle human mind moved on to the next thing. The only prayers Selene ever received—and it had been some years— were from random witches who used the Moon Goddess's name as an archetype during spell casting.

She closed her eyes and listened. *Esteemed Selene, Moon Goddess of Greece, I pray to you with an open heart and a free mind. My spirit hath hope to reach you during yonder dark days of peril and misery...*

Astonished, the lunar deity opened her eyes wide, then met her brother's inquisitive gaze. "It's that young witch who made the earth tremble, the ley line rider. Sybil, the one who challenged Umaq in Machu Picchu. She wants to come to Athens and fight for us!"

"You mean the witch who made the earth bleed when she ruptured the ley line," Helios responded in a frown. "She failed against Umaq, and Inti is dead. What makes you think she can help me?"

"Helios, we don't have much choice," Selene pleaded. "I can truly feel the selfless aura and courage around that girl. Together, we may have a chance."

Encouraged by the prayer, she thought of the *Homeric Hymns*, an ancient collection of thirty-three Greek hymns dedicated to individual gods. Crafted in dactylic hexameter, as are the "Iliad" and "Odyssey", some historians have credited these hymns to the poet Homer.

Selene smiled as she thought of hymn thirty-two, the one written just for her: *And next, sweet voiced Muses, daughters of Zeus, well-skilled in song, tell of the long-winged Moon. From her immortal head a radiance is shown from heaven and embraces earth; and great is the beauty that ariseth from her shining light. The air, unlit before, glows with the light of her golden crown, and her rays beam clear, whensoever bright Selene having bathed her lovely body in the waters of Ocean, and donned her far-gleaming raiment, and yoked her strong-necked, shining team, drives on her long-maned horses at full speed, at eventime in the mid-month: then her great orbit is full and then her beams shine brightest as she increases. So she is a sure token and a sign to mortal men.*

"I will send my moon chariot to Salem, Helios," she said, thinking of her strong-necked, shining team of horses wearing their long manes. The lovely hymn had depicted her steeds perfectly. She offered her brother a determined nod. "Sybil and her friends will come. We are deities, but I believe our fate lies in the hands of a mortal."

About the Author

Alexander Fernandez was born in Santa Monica, CA and grew up in Rancho Cucamonga. Retired from the United States Air Force after serving 24 years, he lives with his wife Helem in Rocklin, CA.

Alex has been writing fantasy and paranormal stories since early childhood for both school and for pleasure. He hopes to make a lasting emotional impact in his readers. He thrives in the exhilaration of creating memorable characters and adventures that become a part of the reader's life.

ADDITIONAL BOOKS BY THIS AUTHOR IN
EPIC FANTASY:

Lonely World Trilogy

Book One: Tears for a World
Book Two: Tears for Love
Book Three: Tears for Life